A

KING IN

DISGUISE

ISBN 978-1-61795-385-9

Published by Worthy Inspired, a division of Worthy Media, Inc.,
134 Franklin Road, Suite 200, Brentwood, Tennessee 37027.

Cover Design by Christopher Tobias
Page Layout by Bart Dawson

Printed in the United States of America

1 2 3 4 5—LBM—18 17 16 15 14

A
KING IN
DISGUISE

A PARABLE

TODD HAFER

WORTHY
Inspired

TABLE OF CONTENTS

INTRODUCTION

Here is an insider's secret about many Christian publishers: They have blacklists. These lists name people who cannot be quoted in the publishers' books, no matter how wise and helpful their quotes might be.

These lists feature people who have failed morally, or who have criticized "the church." Do not point out that the latter criterion would exclude Jesus himself. Publishers will not be amused. Trust me on this.

Søren Kierkegaard, who wrote the parable that inspired the novel you are about to read, should be on all these blacklists. Few people blasted the church and organized religion with as much consistent vigor as the Danish philosopher and thinker. He contended that his country's dominant church, the Danish Lutheran Church, contained "no true Christians." Later in his life, he ceased attending church and encouraged others to do likewise. On his deathbed, he refused Communion.

Kierkegaard detested corporate-style religion. He asserted that God wants honesty, not conformity. God wants an authentic personal relationship with each one of his people. He does not want any army of clones. Yes, clones never criticize the church, but they are afraid to live honestly before their Lord.

On his headstone, Kierkegaard chose these words:

In yet a little while . . .

Then the whole fight

Will all at once be done

Then I may rest . . .

And perpetually

Speak with my Jesus.

This story portrays a God who desires from each of us a love that is free and voluntary. He desires a unique relationship with each of us. A relationship based on the love that naturally flows from heart to heart as we walk side by side with our Lord.

This is the kind of God that Søren Kierkegaard served. This is the kind of God we should all serve. You can quote me on that.

Todd Hafer

CHAPTER 1

ATTACK OF THE TRIAD

The sharp-boned man with the black teeth was Roth. He breathed cheap ale into Johannes's face when he snarled, "All your money now, or you will be more holes than man."

Roth brandished a short sword in his right hand. The sword was well-made, probably Dutch, Johannes surmised. But it had not been well-cared for. It was grimy and littered with nicks. Its edges looked dull. It had probably not seen a whetstone in a longer time than Roth had seen a dentist.

Johannes studied the hand that held the sword. It was trembling slightly. He knew a few tales of Roth, shared with him by the king's knights. Roth had lived at least forty-five years, and he looked ten years beyond that. He was a man too old, and usually too drunk, to be a highwayman. At least a successful highwayman.

Beside Roth stood a plump man with bloodhound jowls and a mashed-in nose. Brooks was his name. Or was it Brookings? He was said to be as powerful as an ox, but he also fought with all the grace and cunning of one. He wore a dagger on his belt, and he wielded a wooden club in his big bear paw of a right hand.

Johannes didn't know the third man, the newest member of the Triad. He appeared to be the youngest of the three. He stood behind his partners. His tar-black hair was coiled tightly against his head. His face was red, like raw steak. Like Brooks, he wore a knife on his belt. The knife's leather grip looked new. Had it ever been used? He seemed to have no other weapon. And he did not seem eager to use the one he had. He was thin. His body showed little possibility of muscle.

Johannes surmised that Red Face must be the replacement for Two-Finger Tomas (formerly known as Four-Finger Tomas and Three-Finger Tomas). Tomas was currently occupying a narrow bunk in the jail of the Upper Kingdom. The Triad's membership was ever changing. Only Roth was a charter member. During the past year alone, the rest of the cast had turned over half a dozen times. Every few months, someone from the Triad was jailed, executed, or converted to faith.

Two years prior, Roth's younger brother had become drunk and tumbled down the steep wooden stairs of the Blackstar Inn. He died of a broken neck. He was on his way down those stairs to fight a local blacksmith, whom he believed to be laughing at his retreating hairline.

Occasionally, the band's number would swell to four, five, or even six, but the name remained Triad. This made them the butt of jokes, but the king's knights had warned Johannes to fear the Triad's mayhem, not its mathematics.

As Johannes sized up the men, he was grateful that the current band's number matched its moniker. It was almost impossible to escape a fight with four men or more without suffering significant injury. Even men as drunk and foolish as these.

He took two steps back from Roth's continuing stream of threats—and his rancid breath.

He stopped when he felt the trunk of a great oak tree against his back. The tree would be his ally, thwarting any attack from behind. Perhaps a branch would deflect a blow from Roth's sword or Brooks's club. Perhaps he could maneuver one of the men to stumble over the large Y-shaped branch lying nearby. When you were outnumbered, almost anything could be your friend. A tree stump. A startled yelp from a passerby. Even a handful of dirt, hurled into an attacker's eyes.

Johannes's own eyes flicked in all directions. Though its membership changed like the seasons, the Triad was known for a few constants. They were full of too much confidence and too much strong drink. But they were as violent as they were greedy. In recent months, they had allegedly killed a man. Allegedly. That was the only reason Roth was not dangling from a noose in the Upper Kingdom's town square. Or settling his square head onto the chopping block at Denton, the Lower Kingdom town where they preferred the axe to the noose when sending criminals to eternal judgment.

For a moment, attackers and victim were still, as if posing for a portrait. But this stillness, Johannes knew, would be fleeting.

A gust of wind drifted over the four men. Then the wind died, leaving an eerie silence. Johannes felt his morning breakfast, a loaf of dark bread with butter and honey, sitting in his gut like a brick. Sparks shot up his spine, as if he were being attacked by wasps.

Johannes knew this feeling like an old dueling partner: Fear. But he didn't fight the fear. He recalled his father's words, repeated year after year: "Do not be afraid to be afraid."

Fear had kept his nerves and reflexes alive. For that matter, fear had kept *him* alive. Through two revolts and the Great Mountain War. Through more duels than he cared to count. And through at least a dozen battles with criminal fools like these.

Johannes struggled to smooth the ripples of fear out of his voice when he spoke. "I have very little money," he offered, meeting Roth's eyes. "Little of anything, to tell the truth. But I will gladly give what I have. Those weapons are not necessary."

"They are," Roth said. He waved his dirty sword in front of his face. "They mean that you will give us *everything*. Starting with whatever is hanging from that thick silver chain around your neck."

Johannes's left hand drifted to his neck. He traced the outline of the silver cross with his forefinger. His right hand gripped his sword, resting in its leather sheath. He freed the cross and let it tumble against his white tunic.

"This cross," he said, dipping his head, "is a gift from my mother. My mother, who is . . . gone now. You can have every coin I have, but you cannot have this. Let me give you my coins, and I will be on my way. I desperately need to continue to my destination."

Roth snorted. He turned his head to speak to Brooks.

Johannes struck. With his left hand, he swatted Roth's dull blade aside. The man's eyes widened. He didn't expect a bare-handed smack on his sword.

Opposite the point of Johannes's rapier rested a round iron pommel, the size of a child's fist. Johannes drew his sword and raised it over his head. He brought the pommel down hard. He caught Roth on the top of his head. He dropped to one knee, howling with pain.

Brooks bent over and tried to wrestle his partner to his feet.

Red Face stepped forward and drew his knife.

Johannes wielded his sword.

In his hand, the sword—a slim and graceful rapier— came alive. A striking viper with razor fangs.

Red Face lunged at him.

Johannes's sword cut through the air with a breathy

whistle. The blow caught the attacker just under the jawbone.

The sword would have separated that florid head from its torso, had not Johannes turned his wrist at the last moment. Thus, the flat of the British steel blade struck Red Face, not its deadly edge. He crumpled to the ground as if his bones had been removed. He lay there, snoring, in a tangle of ropy limbs.

Meanwhile, Brooks had helped Roth stand. Roth squared off with Johannes once more, a lion snarl on his face. But he was swaying slightly, like a fern in a strong wind. Johannes lowered the point of his sword to the bandit's great bulging belly.

"One move," he warned, "and we will all soon discover what you enjoyed for breakfast."

Roth's angry face fell away like a cheap party mask.

"On your knees," Johannes commanded.

Roth swallowed and nodded his great brick of a head once. With some clumsy effort, he settled his knees in the dirt.

"Your sword," Johannes said.

Roth looked up at him, then laid his sword carefully on the ground. Johannes grabbed it and flung it like a discus into the trees.

Johannes then swung his head toward Brooks, the flat-nosed thief. He had taken a few steps back and was struggling to wrestle his knife from its sheath with his left hand while holding his club in his right.

"Stop," Johannes said.

The man bellowed with indignation and, with a mighty tug, freed his knife.

He charged, with flaming eyes. With his knife hand, he thrashed wildly at Johannes's throat. Johannes ducked. The knife cut an arc well above his head.

Johannes rose, deftly thrusting forth the heel of his left hand. He struck Brooks on the bridge of his mashed nose. He felt the crunch of cartilage.

The man dropped both of his weapons and sunk to his knees. He covered his wrecked nose with both hands. He snorted and snuffled like a truffling hog. When he removed his hands, Johannes saw blood leaking from both nostrils. Johannes almost felt sorry for him. Almost.

Johannes sheathed his sword. He stepped back to Roth, grabbed him by both shoulders, and yanked him to his feet. Then he held him firmly, as if he were a crooked painting that needed straightening.

Roth's eyes were cloudy and leaking at the corners. "Are you going to kill me?" he asked. "Kill us all?"

"I hope I will not have to," came the answer. "I have not needed to kill anyone in weeks. It would be nice to keep my blade clean. But, if you wish to live to see tomorrow, understand this: The Triad is over. Stay off of these footpaths. Stay out of the alleys of Denton and Bolsta and Hartwell. Learn to farm. Learn to juggle. Learn a new trade. Or you will die. Soon. If we meet again, pray that it will not be at the point of my sword."

Roth parted his cracked, flaking lips. "You will be our executioner?"

Johannes released Roth. "Perhaps. But what is sure is that I will be your king. Someday soon. My name is Prince

Johannes, of the Two Kingdoms. I know you have heard of me. Son of Morgan the Merciful. But if you ever stand before me in the Hall of Judgment, do not expect mercy."

Johannes shoved Roth hard, and he tumbled to the ground again.

"I don't understand," Roth said. He seemed close to tears. "You do not dress like a prince. You look like no prince I've ever seen."

Johannes's head bobbed up and down. "I hear that a lot," he said.

And then Johannes proceeded down the footpath, toward a small house that held his future. As he walked, he shook out his sword hand, which was buzzing like it was full of bees. *The price of striking to warn, not to kill,* he thought. Being the son of Morgan the Merciful came with a price.

The wind was gathering strength again. It sounded like a whining dog. The Lower Kingdom town of Denton was still a mile away, and word was that, these days, only fools and criminals frequented the footpaths between the Upper and Lower Kingdom.

Johannes smiled. "Only fools and criminals," he whispered. "And the odd king-to-be."

CHAPTER 2

SHELTER FROM
THE STORM

After another quarter hour on the footpath, Johannes veered east, away from the footpath, and found the main road to Denton. He stepped carefully, minding the deep ruts left by the carts drawn by oxen or horses. You could snap an ankle bone if you did not mind your step. After several tedious minutes of picking his way, he abandoned the road for the footpath, which followed the same general course to Denton, albeit with more maddening turns.

The footpath was bordered by trees and dotted with large rocks, crouching like panthers. Ideal hiding places for highwaymen eager to relieve travelers of their gold, their cloaks, and, sometimes, their virtue. Johannes ran a finger along the swept-metal hilt of his rapier. The steel was as fine as a princess's skin.

He didn't expect another encounter this day, but if one came he was ready.

Two days prior, winter had returned for what Johannes hoped was one last dance. Snow fell, then melted. Great whacks of the footpath were a gummy black mess. The sun was out this morning, but it was small and pale and cold as a stone.

The trees he passed as he stepped around the worst of the mud were leafless and skeletal. Gaunt as beggars. And there was no sign of the jade spring grasses that his mother had loved.

As Johannes drew closer to Denton, he drifted by a large pasture, more brown than green.

In the pasture, a band of massive work horses stamped their hooves nervously. One of them raised its head and whinnied. Johannes smiled and nodded in return.

Near the horses, flies buzzed lazily around a horse pie the size of a cart wheel.

Just ahead of him, a wild dog bounded up a bald hill and sniffed the air. Johannes sniffed too, and the wind brought the fragrance of the moist earth to his nostrils. Soon, he would smell Denton. And that was at once a blessing and a curse.

Denton was a nameless little village to most of the world. The smallest of the three towns that made up the Lower Kingdom. And the most despised.

Hundreds of years before, limestone was discovered in the area. Eventually, a small community developed around the quarries, which were overseen by a towering man named Eron Denton. Most of the community's inhabitants were quarriers and their families.

As time passed, the limestone supply dwindled. The town, by then known as Denton, feared for its survival. And so the citizens allowed surrounding communities, including the sister cities of Bolsta and Hartwell, to use their abandoned quarry pits for the discarding of animal carcasses and other assorted garbage. For a reasonable fee.

Within a century, Denton was known for one thing: Garbage. More than half of its population worked at the disposal sites, or supported those who did. There was gold in garbage. The average Denton resident out-earned one from Bolsta or Hartwell by 25 percent.

But the financial success came with baggage. Foul and rotting baggage. To many people in the Upper and Lower Kingdoms, Denton was a joke. Mothers told their children, "Go bathe. You smell like Denton!"

Passing gas was known as "leaking a Denton."

A few of the more cruel residents of the neighboring towns would greet a Dentonite by extending one hand and plugging their noses with the other.

The city was mocked, but it was also feared, as a breeding ground for disease. "Denton Disease" became a catch-all for illnesses that ravaged the body and the mind.

Johannes heard the low rumble of thunder and looked skyward. A battalion of black clouds was forming. A gust of wind rushed at him, and he felt danger on its breath.

The smallest of the skeletal trees along the footpath bowed to this wind.

And then the storm hit, in full force. As sudden as a robbery in an alley. Rain blew at him sideways, whiplashing his face.

He ducked his head and quickened his step. Moments later, an icy blast caught him face-on and left tiny ice crystals in his well-trimmed cinnamon beard.

Johannes shook his head. Why did *cold* rain always fall the hardest? His eyes began to water, and the tears froze against his skin. He covered his ears with his hands, hoping to give himself a modicum of warmth.

He groaned when he tried to adjust his leather scabbard so he could walk more freely. His hands were bruise-purple and stubborn in their movements. *If the Triad attacked me now*, he thought, *I would be as helpless as a newborn.*

He wrapped his arms around himself, not caring how ridiculous it must look. This was not the posture of a king-to-be. This was the pose of a cold and scared child who needed his mother.

After several minutes, he felt that the storm was robbing him of everything that made him a man. He wanted to break into a run, like a race horse in the home stretch. Run until he found the house he sought—or until he froze and dropped dead on the footpath.

Presently, the rain turned to snow. The wind gathered even more strength.

He felt his teeth rattling like dice in a cup. His breath made round white clouds that grew larger with every few steps.

Then he saw it. The old farmhouse built of heavy stones and mud. Roof thatched with leaves, straw, and heather.

A coil of gray smoke rose from the chimney.

The royal messengers had found the house for him and provided a detailed description of the building and the surrounding property. To Johannes, this was the most important house in the Two Kingdoms, because it was *her* house.

The gathering snow muffled his footsteps as he turned on the narrow walkway that led to the front door. He wondered if his crunching footfalls could be heard inside. He stopped at the front door and rapped urgently with frozen knuckles. He was embarrassed at how bad it hurt. He had punched drunks in a tavern with less discomfort. Taverns were warm. So, usually, were drunks.

He wondered if Regine would jump in her seat at the sound of his fist on her thick wooden door. He stamped his frozen feet and tried to will away the shivering.

The door opened with a weary groan. There she stood, staring at him wordlessly. Hair red as embers, eyes dark as plums.

Backlit by the pale sun, Johannes wondered if she would recognize him. Perhaps she would not recognize him in any light. It had been at least a fortnight since they met.

"May I be entering?" he asked her. His voice was high and soft, but he knew his question did not sound like a question. More like an announcement, perhaps even a proc-lamation. Monarchs were not skilled at asking questions, unless they were rhetorical, or accusatory.

"Who are you?" Regine said. "And why are you here?" Her voice was as sharp as cut glass. And as beauti-ful. Johannes allowed himself a fleeting smile. *Her* ques-tions did not sound like questions either. They were ac-cusations. Maybe even verdicts. Like those his father issued in the Great Hall. The kind of verdicts *he* would issue one day. When he was King Johannes, Ruler of the Two Kingdoms.

"I am cold," he said. Not much of an answer to either of Regine's queries.

"It's a cold morning," she observed, with a roll of those dark eyes. "Unwise for walking alone, with no cloak. No gloves. No cap."

Johannes looked down at his white linen shirt and brown canvas pants, both soaking wet and tight against his skin. He wore thin leather shoes, with no stockings. He shrugged helplessly.

She tapped a forefinger against her temple. "Are you . . . are you daft?" she half-whispered.

Johannes felt his head bob affirmatively.

"Perhaps," he said. "But mostly I am simply cold. Five minutes by your fire could save my life." He held out both hands, so she could see them shaking.

Regine did not move. She continued to block the threshold. "You still haven't told me who you are," she said. "Or where you have come from. How am I to know if your life is worth saving by my fire?"

He shivered and stamped his frozen feet. "That is fair," he said. "I know that I owe you an explanation. And explain I will."

He pulled in a shaky breath of the frozen air. He knew that if he answered honestly, she would think he was lying. *He* would almost think he was lying. So he told an actual lie: "I was traveling with a troupe of performers, but we were attacked on the road. I ran away, and, well, here I am. Seeking only safety and a bit of warmth. Then I will be on my way."

He looked down at his swept-hilt rapier in its

handsome scabbard. It might as well be a banner that proclaimed LIAR.

"It must have been awkward," Regine said, "to run away so fast with that sword smacking against you and encumbering your legs. Is that weapon part of your act, trouper? Are you a sword-swallower? Or can you carve pagan idols—or perhaps small woodland animals—out of cedar or chestnut with that blade?"

She stood with her fists on her hips, her eyes boring into him.

Johannes closed his eyes for a moment. A young European princess, who had almost become his wife, deemed his eyes "the promising blue of a morning sky." But that princess was across the ocean now. With a brown-eyed warrior from the North Lands.

That princess was not like *this* woman. This woman who used words like darts. And her aim was true. She hadn't missed him once. If only the princesses who visited him in the Upper Kingdom were half as smart, or half as beautiful, as this. If only they challenged his wits like this.

He opened his eyes. He glanced past Regine's shoulder to the interior of the house. A fire burned in a black stone hearth, spreading its welcome heat.

An old iron kettle hung over the flames. The fire, like blue-orange liquid, curled around the kettle's round black bottom.

The firelight glowed on the face of a leathery old man who sat nearby, in a high-backed wooden chair. His hair was as white and wispy as summer clouds. The lines in his face were deep, as though an engraver's tool had etched them.

The old man was frowning into the fire. Perhaps it had offended him by burning too hot and bringing saltwater to his eyes. He drank hungrily from a large earthenware mug. With each sip, the frown seemed to fade a bit.

He turned to stare at Johannes. He raised his mug. "Mead, of my own making," he said. "I call bees 'God's angels in miniature,' you know. Their honey, I call 'heaven's nectar.'"

Regine shot the old man a sharp glance. He snorted and sipped his mead again. "Close the door, please," he said.

"I do not care which side of the door the frozen stranger will occupy, but this fire is not hot enough to heat the great Denton countryside. For what it is worth, I like the cut of him. He is a liar, but not a good one. Men who are mostly honest make terrible liars. Perhaps his brain is frozen. When it thaws, I wager we will discover some truths."

Regine took two small steps backward. She exhaled forcefully and met Johannes's eyes. "Well?" she said. "A few words of truth will earn you a few minutes by our fire. Or you can be on your way. The choice is yours. Just do not freeze on our property."

"Fair enough," he said with a shiver. "I will explain. If I could just . . ." Regine exhaled impatiently and gestured toward the fire.

Johannes carefully stepped past her. Like a bully, she shoved the door roughly and it thumped shut.

The old man rose, with a great simian grunt. He set his mead on the wooden table that commanded most of the front room. He moved to the fire and stirred the embers with an iron poker. He went about the task with great care.

"A fire is like a woman," he said. "It will burn out if you fail to tend to it carefully."

Regine muttered something that Johannes could not decipher. She looked at the old man and wagged her head slowly. The look on her face was a curious mixture of pity and embarrassment and love. She took a seat on the floor, on a sheepskin close to the fire. She shivered and pulled a quilt around her shoulders.

"Father," she said, "you talk too much. Especially when the mead loosens your tongue. And your brain."

The old man reclaimed his mug from the table and raised it in his daughter's direction. He winked at her.

Regine drew the best qualities from her ancient father. He bequeathed to her the cheekbones that were high and sharp. Those dark-ale eyes. Small and delicate ears that hugged either side of her head.

Johannes guessed that Regine had her mother to thank for the proud nose and the fiery hair that grew as thick and wild as brambles.

He did not see any signs of that mother, or of anyone

else. There was a small narrow bed to the left of the hearth. He could see a small bedroom on the other side. That was the house, in total.

Regine pointed to a chair pushed under the table. "There," she said. Johannes wondered what it would be like when he was addressed as something other than an unruly child or untrained dog.

He sat down and flexed his fingers. They writhed like earthworms in the sun.

The father yawned and rose from his fireside chair again. He lumbered to the table and sat opposite Johannes.

"I would covet a look at that sword," he said. He offered both palms to Johannes.

Johannes hesitated for a moment. "It is mainly for show," he said. "I have found that it discourages thieves and other troublemakers. I prefer to solve problems without violence. I am not much for fighting. I prefer wisdom and patience to this," he said, patting his sword like a faithful dog.

"That is intriguing," the old man said. "Now, may I see your mainly-for-show weapon?"

Johannes unsheathed his rapier and placed it gently in the old man's hands.

Regine's father ran his hands lovingly over the sword, from the tip of the blade to the iron pommel at the opposite end. "Double-edged," he said softly. "A handsome cut-and-thrust weapon. Versatile."

He grasped the sword's handle, rotating his arm first one way, then the other. "Swept hilt, skillfully crafted," he said. "Good protection for your hand. And good for trapping an opponent's blade in its steely web. Then he is at your mercy. For a blow from your fist. Or a stab from your dagger."

Johannes cleared his throat nervously.

"Fine steel," the man said. "Not local, I would wager. Spain, perhaps? Even the Far East? It's not Damascus steel, of course. You are not going to slice through an opponent's sword or anything like that. But still . . ."

"It's British steel," Johannes muttered. "It was a gift."

"I hope you thanked the giver profusely," the old man said. He ran a puffy finger over the sword's crosspiece, then the handle.

"Wire-wrapped grip, padded with leather," he added with an admiring whistle. "I bet it never slips, during your . . . performances. Trouper."

Regine was at the table now, standing over her father's shoulder and studying the sword. "Is this what all the finer traveling minstrels are carrying these days?" she asked. "Swept-hilt rapiers? Deadly weaponry to complement their lutes and costumes and fancy hats with dyed plumes? Who, I wonder, gives a gift like this to a performer?"

The old man cleared his throat. With both hands, he handed the sword to Johannes, like a nanny returning an infant to its mother. "I noticed a smear of blood under the crosspiece," he said. "Rather fresh blood. And yet— you are not bleeding. Unless you are leaking from some unseen place."

Johannes swallowed hard.

The man leaned back in his chair as he watched

Johannes sheath his weapon, soft as a whisper. "I noticed a few nicks and dings," he said. "But your blade is wearing gracefully. You are taking good care of it. Nice crisp edges, just as they should be. Bone, after all, is hard. So are steel-rimmed shields. Even chain mail is sturdy stuff. Of course, if one is skilled enough to strike the neck, the hands, or the legs, the damage to the rapier is minimized. The legs are best, I think. Large targets, but usually poorly protected. The legs are a long way from the brain. They are the last to get the messages, aren't they? Of course, because this sword of yours is rarely used, *that* could explain its superb condition." He leaned forward and shot a long steel stare at Johannes.

Then the old man pushed his chair away from the table and wobbled to the front window. He stared into the fierce storm. He addressed Johannes without turning to him. "What did you tangle with out there, young man? Whose blood hides on your blade? Did you encounter a wolf? A great bear, perhaps? Or something more sinister?"

The old man cleared his throat again, to little avail. His voice was as thin and as ragged as a beggar's clothes.

"We do not get many visitors here," he said. "Few passersby, human or otherwise. Only ghosts these days. Always only ghosts." He stared outside for a few moments more. Then he returned to the table and dropped back into his chair. "I am Truman, by the way," he said. "In case you are wondering."

Johannes reached across the table and extended his hand, which still felt half-frozen. Truman offered his hand as well. The hand that Johannes shook was puffy and rough to the touch, like the pads of an old hound's paw.

The old man looked frail, but he possessed a grip like a steel trap. He squeezed Johannes's hand and gave it a sharp twist as well.

"I am pleased to meet you, Truman," Johannes said. "My name is Climacus." *My middle name is Climacus*, Johannes thought.

"That is a fine sword, Climacus," Truman said. "For duels. And for self-defense. But when it comes to battle, give me an axe. Give me a mace, a pike, a lance, or a spear. For the love of the Vikings, give me a war hammer!"

Johannes caught himself nodding. Bastien, the knight who taught him the art of battle, loved the war hammer.

"All you say is true," Johannes said. "But the rapier is a versatile weapon. Easy to command, with practice. And the rapier seems to have a nose for finding any chink in the armor, or flaw in the chain mail."

Johannes saw that the old man was eyeing him with suspicion. "At least, that is what I have been told," he added quickly.

Then the house grew quiet, save for the snapping fire and the occasional rumble and gurgle from Truman's bulging round belly.

Presently, Regine moved to the kettle and poked at its contents with a large wooden spoon.

"It's dead. I promise," her father assured her.

"I have better hopes for the partridge who gave his life for this stew," she said, "than simply *dead*."

Johannes felt a great gust of wind shake the house. The smoke struggled to creep up the narrow stone chimney. He looked out the lone window. It was so dark that he wondered if the sun had become confused and tucked itself behind the high mountains of the Upper Kingdom.

He could almost feel the stormy darkness pressing in on the walls.

Regine went to the cupboard and grabbed three small wooden bowls. He watched her ladle the stew into each one. She served her father first. She sat opposite him at the table and shoved a bowl toward him, as if the bowl had offended her. She moved Johannes's bowl to him with a playful nudge.

Then she bowed her head. Johannes bowed his head, too, but he kept his eyes open. He watched her lips form a prayer that he could not hear.

What a strange power this young maiden possessed! You saw it, yes, but you also felt it. Johannes did not fear any of the exotic princesses he had met, courtesy of his royal birth. He did fear soldiers and bandits, like the Triad—especially when they were armed and drunk and reckless. But he feared a sharp word from Regine as much as he feared a blow from Roth's clumsy and dull short sword.

The stew was littered with stringy fowl, chunks of

potato, and a few slivers of fatty bacon. But it was steaming hot and cleverly spiced. It bit like a playful puppy.

"This is good," he said, smiling into his bowl. "Thank you so much."

"I hope it will help you warm up," she said. "And help you warm up to the truth. The truth about who you are. I will help you get started. You didn't say anything about being a performer when you visited our inn, the Blackstar last month. By the way, we own it, my father and I.

"Anyway, you were polite and kind. You asked my name, and you always called me Regine. Not woman. Or wench. Or worse. Thus, I did not have to spit in your stew or blow my nose in your ale. And you gave me a generous tip. But you did not give me your name. You stumbled over your own words, like a drunk, trying to keep from spilling that particular secret."

Johannes felt his eyes grow wide. "Do you remember all your guests so well?"

She allowed herself a fleeting smile. "Not all of them. But, as I said, you were kind. A gentleman. Those are rare enough to stick in one's mind."

"I remember you, too," he said. Immediately he wished he could retrieve the words.

"I hear that all the time. Men, it seems, remember me. Especially the drooling sloppy men who have had too much ale or cheap wine."

Johannes placed a hand over his heart. "I have had no ale all day," he said.

She looked at him as if he were rotted food. "All day?" she asked. "And here it is almost noon! You should be knighted. Perhaps if I could borrow your sword . . ."

"Regine!" the old man coughed.

Johannes quickly finished his stew. He rose. "Thank you for the dinner," he said. "And the . . . warmth. I must—"

Regine waved her hand like a banner, cutting him off.

"Sit," she commanded. "I will heat some spiced cider. You are not escaping here without a better story than Forlorn Trouper in Peril. When you dined at our inn, your eyes were everywhere. You took in everything. Like a spy. Or perhaps an aspiring thief."

CHAPTER 3

NAKED TRUTHS?

Johannes sipped from the mug of steaming cider that Regine had poured for him.

"Good?" Regine asked him, arching her eyebrows.

"Like liquid heaven."

"My mother's recipe," she said sadly.

Johannes waited for further explanation. None came.

She bent over her mug of cider, as if trying to protect it from something.

"I come from the Upper Kingdom," Johannes offered. "And I am no trouper. I am sorry for the subterfuge. I am just a simple laborer. I was embarrassed to admit it. Back home, work has become scarce of late, so I have been seeking work in the Lower Kingdom."

Regine aimed a slender forefinger at his head. "That," she said, "is the story I heard you telling an old soldier from Bolsta at the inn last month. He sat next to you, at the middle plank table."

Truman belched happily and turned toward Johannes. "The Upper Kingdom, eh? Have you done any of your simple labor inside the castle walls?"

Johannes let the question roll around his head, like a marble in a jar. "Not lately," he said. "Perhaps King Morgan cannot afford me anymore."

"Perhaps you do such good work that it lasts and lasts," Truman offered. "You look like a young man who enjoys work. Ah, youth! If I had known how temporary it is, I would have savored it more."

"Besides," Regine said, "if the old feckless king needs

more gold, he can just levy another tax on the harvests and the merchants. After all, it has been almost a year. It's time for him to thrust his greedy hand into the small pockets of the working class once again. That's what's coming. You shall see."

Johannes winced in spite of himself. Regine's speech made his heart shrink like a prune in his chest. Her words about his father, Morgan the Merciful, gored him like a horn. He knew that people in both kingdoms often referred to him as Morgan the Mercenary. But they just didn't understand.

"I haven't heard anything of another tax," he said. He nibbled his lower lip and searched his mind. He searched his heart. *Was this the first true thing he had said since entering this home?*

He cleared his throat. "Who has told you of an impending tax?" he asked. "Surely not Denton's chancellor— or one of the king's messengers."

Truman laughed humorlessly. "You know how life works in the one-church towns like Denton. The rumors fly, swift and thick, like arrows from the king's archers. You cannot go anywhere without being pierced by one."

Johannes sipped hungrily from his mug of tart cider. "To be fair," he said, "many, many people are in the king's employ, both directly and indirectly. As a laborer, I caught a glimpse of how many families could be affected when kingdom jobs are lost. I surmise that the question to tax or not to tax greatly vexes our king."

Regine sighed dramatically. Truman patted her hand.

"I will say this on behalf of Morgan Two," the old man said. "He never became fat or ridiculous. Like his father did. Like almost all kings do. That is, if we can trust the portrait that hangs in the chancellor's meeting hall. The king looks like he could still take up a sword or a lance and meet an invading band of pirates."

"He was a fierce warrior," Johannes said, adding quickly, "Or so I have been told."

"He has been like a god to many of us in the Lower Kingdom," Truman said. "To some, the only difference between King Morgan and God is that we have oil portraits of the former. The latter remains a mystery, in oh-so-many ways. Perhaps God is too large to capture, for the painters or the poets."

"Mystery," Johannes echoed the word. "I wonder if that is why Denton has only one church, and it is scarcely bigger than the tannery. It seems that few Dentonites worship."

"Ha!" Regine said. "Trouper—or is it Laborer now?— everybody in Denton worships. Everybody in the Two Kingdoms worships. It is only a matter of what we *choose* to worship."

Johannes nodded.

"I would visit the Church of Denton more frequently," Truman interjected, "if the vicar prayed better."

Regine's eyes widened. "What do you mean, Father? How does one pray better?"

Truman tapped a forefinger on the table, as if trying to establish a beat. "The good Reverend prays with much conviction," he said slowly, "but with very little faith. And he recites Scripture as if he is angry at every blessed word."

Johannes finished his cider. He pushed himself away from the table and rose. "I thank you both for your kindness. For the warmth of your fire. And the warmth of your company."

Regine rolled her dark eyes again. She half-turned, to face the window. "At least you have outlasted the storm," she observed. "Now your journey can continue. Wherever it takes you. And for whatever reason."

Those final words hung in the air like smoke.

"Where will your journey end, Climacus?" Truman asked. "Were you headed to Denton, or away from it, when the storm chased you to our door?"

Johannes thought for a moment. "To Denton," he said. "To look for work. Of course, I have heard that the Blackstar needs a laborer."

"You have heard that, have you?" Truman asked.

Johannes smiled at him. "You know how it is in the cities of the Lower Kingdom: Rumors fly like sparrows."

"Arrows," Regine corrected.

"Touché," Johannes said.

"Spoken like a true swordsman," Truman observed.

Johannes shifted his feet. "I am a hard worker. I can provide testimonials, if needed."

Regine stood and moved to her father's side. She stooped and whispered into his ear for at least a full minute. He frowned at first, but then he drew in a deep breath and nodded his head.

Regine straightened herself. "A man named John oversees the Blackstar for us," she said evenly. "Report to him as soon as you can. If he likes the cut of you, we will have a new laborer. There is a small room above the dining area. You may live there—pending John's approval, of course. He will tell you what your wages will be. If they are not satisfactory to you, you are welcome to seek work elsewhere. The Whetstone is forever hiring, or so it seems. It must be hard to manage a business that does not know whether it wants to be an inn or a brothel."

Johannes felt his face color. "Tomorrow, then?" he said.

"Yes. That will be fine." Regine did not look at him. Instead, she focused on clearing the dishes from the table.

Johannes took two steps toward the door. "When you say laborer . . ." he said.

"Think of it this way," Regine began, "if the Blackstar buys itself a pet pig to entertain our guests, you will be faithfully following that pig with a shovel. Are we clear now, as to the definition of *labor*?"

Johannes shifted his feet. "Of course," he said. "But I should point out that I am a *tektōn*. I have some skills. I am something of a carpenter."

"Good," Regine said, removing the last of the dinner dishes. "Perhaps our pet pig will need a pen built for him. *Tektōn*."

Johannes took another step toward the door.

Regine slid to his side. "Let me show you to the door, Climacus the Laborer."

She smelled of rose water and woodsmoke. She threaded her lean arm through his. He hoped she could not see how this move stunned him. He wondered if his heart had stopped momentarily.

They moved to the entryway. Johannes smiled when he

saw the fat shadows the two of them threw against the wall near the door.

Regine opened the door for him. Her eyes were locked on his shoes, not his eyes, when she spoke: "Travel safely, Climacus. The roads are dangerous now. Even for a laborer with a sharp sword."

Standing at the threshold, he bowed to both of his guests. "Again," he said, "thank you." He began the walk into Denton. He heard the door shut behind him. This time, it closed as softly as a kiss.

CHAPTER 4

THROWING GOLD

Johannes walked swiftly, footsteps crunching through a wet carpet of snow and dead leaves. The sky was hard and gray.

He thought about retracing his steps to the Upper Kingdom, but his clothes, which had been soaked, and then dried by Regine's fire, felt one size too tight. And he did not want to arrive at the palace covered with road dust and smelling of sweat. More than that, however, he was exhausted. He felt that his bones had been drained of their marrow.

In Denton, he would find the chancellor, who would send for the Royal Guard. They would arrive, either with an extra horse, or one of the royal carriages. He could be home within the hour.

At Johannes's request, his father sent Bastien for him. The finest swordsman in the entire kingdom. The man entrusted to teach King Morgan's only son the art of the sword. The art of war. Bastien brought him an extra horse and insulted him only a little when he saw his disheveled state.

Soon, the two men were crossing the Downing River via an ancient stone bridge, wide enough for a parade.

As the Upper Kingdom came into view. Johannes rose in his stirrups. Bastien's free hand moved to his sword. "Anything?" he asked.

Johannes studied the terrain ahead. He shook his head. "Just a ghost," he muttered. "Always only ghosts."

"Jumpy, are we?"

"My stomach feels like it is full of hopping frogs," he said. "Perhaps I picked up the Denton fever."

"You have certainly picked up something. But I am not sure it is a fever. At least not Denton fever. I know who you visited. And I believe I know *why*."

Johannes shot a sharp look at Bastien. Both grew quiet. Their horses' hooves thrummed hollow on the turf that led to the palace walls.

Johannes bathed and ate a simple supper: a loaf of hearty dark bread with butter and honey, along with a glass of milk, still warm from the cow.

Afterward, he went outside and wandered in the ghostly blue twilight. He found a stone bench in one of the well-manicured courtyards and sagged onto it. He sat for a while, listening to the far-off birdsong, and thinking of Regine.

He considered walking to the large lake just outside the palace walls. The moon was full, and he loved the way it threw silver splashes on the water's smooth surface. And he liked to guess at how much gold and silver lay at the bottom of that lake. Riches that he and his father placed there. But it was late. He needed to talk to his father, the king, and King Morgan would not be awake much longer.

Johannes entered the Great Hall through the massive arched front doorway. The room was long and high, paneled in cedar. The ceiling's wood beams were black and as shining as obsidian. He gazed up at the high, wide windows that welcomed both the daylight and the moonshine. He let his hand drift across one of the great stone pillars— pillars that even the towering Bastien couldn't get his arms around.

The room had seen weddings and trials. Performances of comedies and tragedies. Grand celebrations attended by kings and queens, harlots and heretics. Ambassadors were welcomed here. And traitors were sentenced to the gallows.

He walked to the end of the hall and sat in the throne, which was carved to the likeness of a great lion. When he was a boy, he thrilled to sit here, placing his hands over the lion's-paw arm rests. Today he felt unsettled. As if he were being forced to wear another man's clothes. A much older man's clothes. He did not sit long on the throne.

Moments later, he found his father in the Council Chambers, which adjoined the Great Hall. King Morgan sat at the head of the massive council table, which was surrounded by high-backed wooden chairs, padded with velvet. The table legs were carved to look like horses' legs.

The old king honked like a goose into a large silk handkerchief. His breathing was like the crumpling of parchment. He had sad brown eyes like an old dog.

"You don't sound well, Father," Johannes said.

"The price of a long life. Infirmity and loneliness."

"You are a great king. Your life has been a success."

"Success can leave a man very lonely. I am a success, I suppose. But an old and lonely success. I still have many dreams, but they are locked inside me. As are my fears and insecurities. The first I cannot share. The latter I dare not share."

Johannes studied the deep creases in his father's face. He was reminded of Truman. He wondered if he and Regine would wear their years like this one day. He doubted that she would be any less beautiful. About himself, he was not so sure.

He unfastened himself from these thoughts when he heard his father clear his throat. "Why can't you share the truth of your heart, sir?" he asked.

The king coughed into a great silver chalice. He allowed himself a sad smile. "My people," he said, "will desert me at the first sign of weakness. I know that. When you are the king, you cannot carry your pain in a leaky cask."

"Are the people of the Two Kingdoms truly that fickle?"

"Is my son the prince truly this naïve?"

King Morgan raised his right hand. It disappeared into the chalice. Johannes frowned. He wondered what lesson his father intended to teach him by dipping his hand into expensive wine.

But when the king removed his hand, it was full of gold and silver, not dripping with wine. The king let the coins slip through his fingers. Some spun and rolled on the table. Others clattered to the floor.

The king smiled at his son. "Do you remember," he asked, "walking to the royal lake with me, with fistfuls of gold and silver in the pockets of our robes?"

"Of course I do. I was shocked the first time you plucked a gold coin and flung it across the lake. It skipped seven times."

"Eight!"

"If you say so, Father. And I still think it's wasteful, you know."

"Perhaps. But how else could I teach you that gold and silver are nothing? They are shiny metals that someone has decided are worth living for, even dying for. But mica catches the sun's light just as ably, at least to my aging eyes. And no one will give you have an iron penny for a barrow full of mica."

Johannes closed his eyes for a moment. "I didn't want to let go of that first gold coin," he said, his voice warming to the memory. "I felt it would stick in my fingers, as if it had been dipped in honey."

"But you did let it go. It dove to the bottom without one skip."

"Yes, but, as the years accumulated, I became more and more skilled at skipping your fortune across the water and sinking it in the mud."

"*Our* fortune, my son. And even that is not true. Our fortune has nothing to do with silver or gold or silk from China. Or cinnamon from the Indies. When your mother became sick, I offered an unspeakable fortune to any doctor, any magician, any sorcerer who could heal her. But I found something that even all my riches could not buy. Not that an army of charlatans was not eager to separate me from my shiny metals."

The king paused for a moment to rub his puffy eyes.

"The irony is that I would trade all that I own," he continued. "All the gold, silver, and all the rest, to have her back in my arms. I would not care if every ounce of my gold melted and flowed to the sea. The only thing I don't want to burn is the library."

"I am reassured to hear that. Some of the best times of my childhood were spent in that library."

"Do you know where my crown is?" King Morgan asked him. "I thought I left it in the library, but it is not there now."

"You have misplaced it again?"

"I believe so. But I want you to find it for me. Because I want to stomp that crown. I want to melt it down and turn it into an ashtray. Perhaps even a chamber pot."

Johannes started to rise from his chair. His father raised his right hand, then lowered it. Johannes settled back down.

The king exhaled slowly. "I would give away all my gold, even bury it all in the bottom of the sea, to have your mother back," he said. His eyes began to leak tears. "I would burn down the entire palace and dance as it turned to ashes. Do you hear what I am saying, my son? Do you *understand* what I am saying?"

"I am trying to."

"Being her husband brought me greater joy than

being king. And it was a more sacred responsibility. Do you hear me?"

Johannes nodded. "I think so, Father."

The king waved his hand dismissively in front of his face, as if swatting mosquitoes. "Do not think," he said. "*Believe.* Everything that is not eternal is rotting, by the second. And only love is eternal. Do not wait to become an old man before you understand these things."

"Yes sir," Johannes said quietly.

He looked at his father's old and kind face. The tears made his eyes glitter.

"I miss her every day," he whispered.

"I miss her, too," Johannes said. "I wish she were here now, so that I could tell her, with you, that I am in love."

The king let his chin droop. "And you unearth this revelation only now, my son? Only after I have emptied my heart before you?"

"I didn't know how to stop you. I didn't know if I should."

"I only wish you would have. Because now I know

there is no way I can talk you out of what I know, and fear, that you are going to do. Tell me I am wrong."

This time, Johannes did rise. He walked to the door. "You are not wrong, my king. I am sorry."

Johannes returned to the arched doorway of the Great Hall. He stood and watched. Small bands of people ambled by the palace. They were watched warily by the Royal Guard. Young and fit men in silver breastplates and fine helmets. He thought of the Blackstar. Protected only by an old door with a bolt lock. But that was about to change. The inn was about to receive additional protection. A protector who had been personally trained by a Royal Guardsman.

CHAPTER 5

DEAD KINGS

Johannes reclined in his massive bed. The walls were covered with portraits of kings past. Kings mostly forgotten. Some done in oils, others in pastel-colored chalk.

All the dead kings seemed to be smirking at him. Even his grandfather, Morgan the First. They all seemed to bear the same message: "This life is wretched, but you dare not complain. From whom do you expect sympathy? To most of your subjects, a king is merely a tyrant in fancy clothing. A clown strutting about with a crown on his head and a silver sword at his side. Meanwhile, his people struggle to find food for that night's supper."

In the morning, one of the staff brought him breakfast—an assortment of sausages, along with a mug of buttermilk and a plate of cheese that smelled like old stockings. Johannes attacked the food as if it were an enemy.

After breakfast, Johannes sat in the library. A fire sizzled and crackled in the small brick fireplace. All four walls were lined with books. He sat at a wooden table, which was covered with an unruly tumble of more books. He marveled that the table did not sag under the weight.

This was his favorite place in the whole kingdom. Here he had tasted and digested the meat of the great books. He often questioned his father about what he was reading. He had longed to question his mother too. But by the time he was reading books whose words outnumbered their pictures, his mother was already a long time gone. Stolen from him by the Great Sickness.

As he sat and read a novel called *The Ghost of the Wolf*,

the spirit of the Upper Kingdom crept into his soul. He knew his city like an expert rider knows his horse, like a faithful woman knows her man.

His father entered the room. He rotated his head first to the left, then to the right.

"There is so much knowledge in these books," Johannes said. "I have tried to keep up with that knowledge for so many years. But I have felt stupid most of the time."

The king nodded.

"So," he said, taking a seat across from his son, "tell me about this woman. The one for whom you want to abandon your kingdom."

Johannes studied his father's cocoa eyes. There he saw a sorrow that was too awful to regard. To look at it for even a few seconds was to risk ruin.

Johannes looked at the pages of his book, without understanding any of the words. "Her name is Regine," he whispered. "To her, I am a person, not a prince. With her, I see the soul shining through her eyes. With so many others—even the princesses who have graced our palace—

I look into their eyes and see almost nothing. All this, and I have spent only a few hours in her company. But I *know*."

"I understand," the king said to his son. "I have lived the same thing."

"I know you have."

"What I do not understand is why you cannot bring her here. What young woman would not want to be a princess? A queen?"

"This one, I am afraid. She has no warm feelings toward the monarchy."

"Are you truly telling me that you intend to leave the Upper Kingdom for good? Our family has occupied the throne for more than five hundred years. You would be the end of that? You know what they say, 'Morgan the Merciful has one heir, but no spare.'"

Johannes nodded his head slowly. "Father, she is the girl of my wildest dreams. This girl with the hair as red as fire. Do you really want me to miss the chance to give those mad dreams a go? Do you want me to die wondering, *What if?*"

"I would not want you to miss that chance. It is awful to miss things. I myself do not miss many things. Save your mother, of course. But I already miss you, Johannes. And you are not yet gone."

"Denton is not that far away, Father."

From the king, came a sad and knowing smile.

"It will be so lonely here without you," he said.

"We will visit often."

Again, the king waved his hand in front of his face. "Do not promise before you understand what you are promising."

"But, Father—"

"No! Listen to me. A great canyon has formed between me and you, Prince Johannes. You feel a hunger that I do not feel. Not anymore. But I remember this hunger. It eats you from the inside. I could forbid you to go. I could forbid your courtship and marriage—if there is to be such things. But I know my son. You would do it anyway. Only you would do it with anger in your heart. Anger toward me. When it comes to love, all roads lead to the same destination. The difference between you and me is sharp now. It has grown sharper each year. It only stands to reason that one of us was going to get cut. How I wish I had never sent you to the Lower Kingdom as my secret scout! It was, perhaps, the worst idea of my life."

Johannes stood and moved to his father's side of the table. King Morgan rose and Johannes hugged him fiercely.

"Some people envy God," the king said. "I do not."

"No?" Johannes formed an *O* with his mouth. After all of these years, his father could still puzzle him.

The king shook his head. "I love God. I would die for Him. But envy Him? No. Never even once."

"I will think on those words on the ride back to Denton."

The king coughed. "Do not think on them too much. Such thoughts hang lines on your face and sprinkle salt in your hair."

Above the Upper Kingdom, the sun was a buttery yellow. Johannes rode to Denton with a smile. He rode with

Bastien to his right and Braithwaite, another member of the Royal Guard, to his left. Both stood over six and a half feet tall. They were called the King's Twin Towers.

Johannes had told them both of his encounter with the Triad the day before. "If they attack today," he said, "it will truly be a fair fight."

"Perhaps not," Bastien said.

Johannes frowned.

Bastien looked at Braithwaite, then brought his horse around 180 degrees. "There is something you should see, Prince Johannes. Or is it Former Prince Johannes?"

Bastien led the way back to the Upper Kingdom's town square. Johannes saw the gallows, made of polished wood, gleaming in the morning light. And he saw Roth, hanging limply by his broken neck. He imagined the drunken criminal, spending the final seconds of his life, squirming and writhing at the end of a coarse rope.

He felt tears pooling in both eyes, though he wasn't sure why. "I tried to warn him," Johannes said. "I shook him like a rag doll and tried to unloose some sense within him."

"There is no warning some men," Braithwaite said.

The three men left the square and rode for a long while in silence.

Halfway to Denton, Bastien cleared his throat. "I must say something. Then I shall be silent about the matter."

Johannes arched his eyebrows. "That would be a first. Please, proceed."

"Your father," he began, "is the best king in the land. He could arrange a marriage to any number of fine princesses. The Upper Kingdom could become twice as rich, and twice as strong, by such a union."

"*Arrange.*" Johannes pronounced the word carefully, as if he had just learned it. "Bas, you cannot arrange true love. I laugh when I see those words standing beside one another on a page: Arrange. Love. You do not arrange love. You fall into it. You tumble headlong. You know you might break your neck, if not your heart. And still, you fall, and you cannot wait to get back on your feet. So that you can tumble again, as soon as you are strong enough."

Bastien wagged his head. "You learned so quickly about the art of the sword, but you are slow to learn about love."

"Really? Do you recall what happened to the last union that my father arranged for me? To a certain princess from the Continent? To a certain princess who sailed away with a warrior from the North Lands two weeks before a royal wedding?"

Bastien closed his eyes for a moment. "I am sorry to revive such pain, Your Grace."

"Do not worry, Bas. Like most of my former loves, she seemed to enjoy liking me. However, she seemed to enjoy disliking me even more."

"Ouch," said Braithwaite.

"There was a time in my life, gents, when I believed marrying a princess was life's ultimate quest. But that was a time when I wore hand-sewn bedroom slippers shaped like mice and my sword was carved from a willow switch."

"Again," Bas said, "I am sorry."

"All is well. I'm sure the pain will stop. When I am dead."

MARTYRS, MAIDENS,
AND MONSTERS

Presently, the three men came to the little clusters of mud huts on Denton's outskirts. When Johannes traveled as an everyman, what he called Going Common, these people shot him the same cold stares they offered to all strangers. Their eyes were dull, but not fearful. He received none of the looks of begrudging admiration he received when he traveled with the royal entourage.

Today, those looks portended suspicion and fear. Like Johannes, Bas and Braithwaite were dressed in common clothes. But all were armed. Besides, there was no hiding the warrior in his two companions. You could dress them as court jesters and still no one would crowd their stool at a tavern, or even cast a disrespectful glance in their direction in church.

The hills just outside Denton were overgrown with weeds as tall as a man. Johannes was tempted to unsheathe his sword and cut them away. But he thought better of it. The rapier sported a fine edge, and his encounter with the Triad hadn't compromised it. So he and the men weaved a serpentine route around the hills.

Denton-proper was a town of rusting iron, splintered wood and rough bricks. A town of one small church, it was home to at least three houses of ill repute. That number did not include the inns that doubled as houses of ill repute. When you dined at one of Denton's taverns, you dined among whores, gamblers, herdsmen, carpenters, and criminals. Among both maidens and monsters. But no saints, and certainly no angels.

Still, at inns like the Blackstar, you might see diners bow their heads and offer thanks before their meal. Perhaps these men and women yearned to be saints, Johannes reasoned. He wondered if they understood that many saints were martyrs first.

Johannes and the Twin Towers arrived at the town's doorstep. He dismounted and handed his horse's reins to Bas. He grabbed his travel sack and looked up at his friends.

"Denton," Bas said. "Smells the same as ever. Like Death just fouled himself."

Johannes laughed politely. "You are good men," he said. "Thank you for helping me to become a good man. Please trust that I know what I am doing here."

"You are following your heart," Braithwaite said. "I understand that. But do not confuse following your heart with knowing what you are doing."

"Touché."

"Spoken like a true swordsman."

At Denton's main street, the dirt path gave way to a road paved with cobblestones.

Perhaps *paved* was too generous a term. The cobblestones were cracked and bruised. The wheels of the oxcarts. The hooves of horses and mules. The heavy boots of sinners and the sandals of saints. All had taken their toll.

Johannes turned when he heard the *slap-slap-slap* of bare feet on the cobbles. *Who would dare go barefoot in this weather?* he wondered. The cobbles felt cold, even through his leather shoes.

It was a boy of about twelve years, running like the devil was chasing him. The boy muttered something to himself as he ran. He smacked shoulders with Johannes as he sprinted by, but he didn't stop to apologize or even acknowledge the incident.

Johannes trudged on, toward his ultimate destination. He stepped through the stomped slush, hands tucked in his pockets.

It was still early morning. Most of the shops on the town's long main street had opened their doors, raised their shutters, and put their wares on display. The potters, the glass blowers, the glaziers, the tanners, and the weavers. Other merchants pushed heavy carts down the street, carts laden with pastries and pottery, blown glass and boiled-meat sandwiches. The most successful of them had a horse or mule to pull their merchandise.

Johannes passed by an old woman peddling hand-woven rugs and two boys selling sweet oranges.

From somewhere up the cobblestone road, Johannes could hear the call of the fishmonger, extolling the virtues of his basket of mackerel. Closer by, butchers and bakers shouted their prices over the hum and bustle of a growing crowd.

Johannes felt his nose assaulted by the aroma of fried pastries, strong beer, and horse manure. And garbage. Heaping pits of garbage.

As he drew near to the Blackstar, Johannes paused at an alley, barely wide enough for two people walking abreast. A small band of men in ragged clothes occupied the alleyway. Bottles were scattered everywhere. One man was crouching on his haunches, retching violently. A boy who couldn't be more than sixteen stood nearby, both palms on a cracked stone wall, dry-heaving. Deeper in the alley, two men lay, one on his back, the other on his stomach.

Johannes smiled sadly. He thought of the Upper Kingdom's Great Hall, after the Harvest Festival, or some similar celebration. Many royal celebrants had lost their dignity, and their supper, in that massive room.

Rich drunks, poor drunks, he thought. They both look equally sad and helpless, whether sick or unconscious in a fine palace or a filthy alley.

CHAPTER 7

THE COFFEE OF
ULTIMATE SADNESS

Johannes stood at the door of the Blackstar. He inhaled deeply and tugged the heavy wooden door open. It protested with a painful groan before giving way to his strength.

He looked back over his shoulder and saw a ghostly gray mist descending over Denton. The mist obscured the mountains of his home. Or was it his *former* home?

He stepped inside the inn and stretched his arms above his head. It had been four days since he had trained with Bastien. And the Triad had not taxed him much. His muscles hungered for action. They felt as soft and soggy as boiled greens.

The Blackstar's main floor was a large open room, furnished with four long plank tables, each with bench seats made of split logs. A huge stone fireplace claimed the room's center. An assortment of pots and kettles hung from iron hooks on the fireplace. Regine had told him that most of the meals were cooked over the fire, though a few dishes were prepared in a small kitchen behind the bar. Even the water for the tea was boiled over the fire.

The Blackstar's other beverages—stout ale, bitter wine, and spiced rum—were stored in fat wooden barrels that lined the room's back wall.

The inn was less than half full on this morning. Some patrons were seated at the long tables. Others leaned against the walls, drinking from tin mugs and eyeing Johannes warily. A group of dangerous-looking men sat in a circle of chairs in the back, huddled together in hushed conversation.

A stout, sad-eyed serving woman drifted from place to place, taking orders. Despite her size, she slipped nimbly among the tables. She moved like a dancer. Or a great predator-cat.

Behind the bar stood John, a thick bear of a man who mixed drinks, directed the staff, and solved any disputes among customers, with the help of a five-pound war sword. His short gray-black hair looked like iron filings standing on end.

He rules the Blackstar like a king, Johannes thought. John directed everything with the force of his will and the great bellows of his lungs.

Johannes adjusted his sword and stepped to the bar. "John?" he said. "Regine told me to seek you out. About the need for a laborer here."

John was carefully polishing the mahogany bar top with a white linen cloth. Johannes began to rest his hands on the bar's gleaming surface, then thought better of it.

"Regine spoke to me too," John said, without looking up from his work. "You are hired. I will have Drenda show you around when things slow down. Do you have a name?"

"It is Jo—it is Climacus," Johannes stammered.

"I see," John said, still not bothering to look up. "Welcome. Climacus. May I offer you something to drink?"

"How is your coffee here?"

John snorted. "If you could brew ultimate sadness," he said, "it would taste like Blackstar coffee. But the stuff works. It will help you work. Just do not drink it late in the evening. You will spend the night watching lizards crawl up the walls. And there are no lizards here."

"I see," said Johannes.

"I can offer you some old wine," John said.

"Very, very old," the serving woman added as she drifted by.

"Some things improve with age, Drenda," John said to her.

"Yes," she said, winking at Johannes. "Some things do."

Johannes waited an hour before business slowed enough for Drenda to give him a tour of the Blackstar.

Drenda had fashioned her obsidian-black hair into a stiff hedge. Her hair provided a stark contrast to her skin, which was as white as a trout's underbelly.

When she spoke, her voice was like molasses, thick and slow and sweet.

She guided Johannes up the arthritic wooden stairs that led from the dining and drinking room to a balcony, which accessed six rooms available for rent. This total did not include the living quarters for the former prince who was now the new laborer for the Blackstar Inn.

"Just there," Drenda said, pointing at a door. "That is your room. Get settled. You will be given a pitcher of drinking water every morning. A bucket of hot water for bathing, and fresh towels every other day. The lye soap will leave your skin rosy and tingling. But do not get it in your eyes."

Johannes nodded.

Drenda knelt and picked up what looked like a crumb of brown bread from the entryway floor. "And if you find you need anything else," she said, "you will need to learn to live with that need."

Johannes reined in a smile. Drenda was as caustic as that lye soap she mentioned, but her words were a refreshing change from all of the "Yes, Your Grace," "As you wish, Your Grace," and "Do you desire anything else, Your Grace?" of the princely life.

This was something new. To be talked to as a person, not a prince. The same way Regine spoke to him.

Drenda turned and headed for the staircase. Johannes began to form a farewell, but she was already halfway down the staircase. He entered his room. A narrow bed sat against the far wall. The bedframe was made of wood that was hand-hewn, although not expertly so. It was topped with a down mattress and a handmade quilt that looked as if it belonged in another century. A century when Morgan the First was king and bronze swords were not uncommon.

The bed linens were crisp and smelled of rosewood. He ran his hand over the bed. The fabric was scratchy as oak bark.

A coal oil lamp burned on a desk near the door. Two stubby candles sat on a nightstand beside the bed. The chamber pot at the foot of the bed was hand-painted with a large pink rose. He found himself grinning at the irony. Some of the royal chamber pots were stenciled with various woodland animals, which made about as much sense as a rose.

There were no portraits on the walls. No carpet on the rough wooden floor.

That rough floor clicked and moaned as he walked across the room. Through his room's one small window, the sun snuck in, creating a blade of light on the floor. He shucked his travel sack off of his shoulder and tossed it on the bed.

Tucked into the room's back corner was a black stone fireplace. He inspected it for a few moments, noting that its grate needed cleaning. Then he returned to the bed to lie down. He noticed a wooden chest at the foot of the bed, next to the chamber pot. It looked like a small coffin. The chest could be sealed with an iron lock, if the lock had not been broken, hanging gamely from one loose screw. He looked inside the chest. It contained an extra set of linens, which smelled of rotting vegetables. He closed the lid. He would fix the chest tomorrow.

There was other work to do first.

CHAPTER 8

A STRANGER IN THE BLACKSTAR

It was five o'clock in the morning. The sun was not up, but Johannes was. He shoveled the fine ashes out of the hearth in the dining hall. He poured them carefully into an iron bucket. Later, he would carry the ashes behind the Blackstar, where Drenda's garden grew. She had told him that the ashes fed her soil, especially hardwood ashes, from the great oaks and yews. Although she would not turn up her nose at softwood ashes, like fir.

Then he carried in armloads of wood for the morning fire. He nurtured that fresh fire, sprinkling twigs into it, as if it were a stew. When the kindling was crackling and sizzling, he grabbed a log as thick as a man's leg and heaved it onto the fire.

He swept the floor and washed down the tables. Then he polished every wooden surface to a wet shine. He had to mop the floor three times before the water in his bucket was not as black as the inn's coffee.

After he topped off the oil in the lamps and trimmed the wicks, Johannes moved to the center of the dining room and turned 360 degrees. He smiled. The Blackstar was so clean that it seemed to glow. He stashed the cleaning supplies in a small closet behind the bar.

The front door opened, framing John's burly figure. A chorus of flies hummed loudly behind him. "Close that door, please," Johannes said. "I have started some porridge in the kitchen, and I don't want those flies getting into it."

"I have tasted your porridge, Climacus. The flies might improve it."

John appeared to be crafting another insult when he was shoved from behind.

"Move, you hulk," Drenda said. "I have work to do."

"Good morning, Drenda," Johannes called. He grabbed his bucket of ashes and headed for the back door. "More food for your garden," he said.

"He's as strong as a plow horse," Johannes heard Drenda say.

"And sometimes about as smart," John answered.

"Give him a chance. It's only been two months."

John began a retort, but Johannes did not linger to hear it.

When he returned to the dining room, John had his hairy arm wrapped around Drenda's barrel waist.

"Is this man bothering you, miss?" Johannes asked.

"Not nearly enough," she said.

John kissed her on top of the head and moved to his place behind the bar.

That night, a Saturday, the Blackstar featured live music. A six-piece instrumental group called the Lonely Dogs set up in front of the bar and delivered a selection of quick and happy songs, each badly played. The Dogs featured shrieking flutes, rattling drums, and the occasional cat-screech from a horn.

The only female member of the ensemble plucked the lyre with clumsy fingers that looked like fat worms. During one of her solos, Regine slid to Johannes's side. "Someone should throw that lyre on the fire," she said. "And do us all a great favor."

Then she leaned into Johannes and they stood together, taking in the ebb and flow of conversation. The sporadic eruptions of drunken laughter. The clinks of bottles. The dull thuds of pewter and tin mugs on the wooden tabletops.

After the band packed up and left, John took his customary place at the head of the center table, like King Morgan addressing the War Council. There, he shared tales of Vikings, pirates, swords-for-hire, highwaymen, and smugglers. He could spin a story like a potter spun his wheel. He created scenes so vivid that Johannes half-expected a band of buccaneers to stumble through the Blackstar's door, pieces of eight in hand, demanding ports of rum.

These stories often ended incredibly, with statements like, "And so I was able to survive for a fortnight, by eating my belt and my shoes, and drinking the blood of toads."

Johannes could feel weariness spreading through his bones like a disease, but he did not want to miss a story. The other men around the table seemed equally enraptured. After each story, many of them would pepper John with questions. After each query, he would stroke his gray-flecked beard and say, "I am glad you asked that."

Usually, that was the spark for the fire of yet another tale.

As the night wore on, John finished a story and pointed a thick finger at Johannes. "Climacus!" he shouted, as if the name were the answer to a most important question. "You come to us from the capital, the Upper Kingdom. Surely you must know some tales. Of great kings, brave knights, and famous spies."

"Well, first of all," Johannes said, "if you are a famous spy, you are doing something wrong!"

This brought a roar from the men.

John drained his mug of ale. "Now you have our attention, so you must tell us a story. It can even be true, if you wish. We are full of much ale and wine. Even the women of Denton are beginning to look rather fine."

Johannes thought for a moment. "I do have a story, John," he said. "And this one is true. Mostly."

He looked around for Regine. He did not see her.

"When I was a laborer for the king," he began, "I was sometimes asked to deliver various important documents throughout the Upper Kingdom. One day, I had so many letters and contracts and bills of sale that I was driven about in one of the royal coaches."

One of the men whistled.

Johannes paused for a moment, then continued. "At one point in our journey," he said, "the coach driver stopped because he feared one of the horses was limping. I got out of the coach to stretch my legs. Suddenly, a strong wind whipped up. It yanked many of the documents from my grasp. Then this evil wind sprayed them toward many assorted compass points.

"The next gust closed the coach door angrily. On my right leg."

One of the men sprayed purple wine across the table.

"Watching all of those papers flutter away, I felt like crying. But this was no time for tears. I started to limp after one particular envelope, which I believed to hold the most important document of all."

"What was it?" John asked. "A marriage certificate?"

"Close," came the answer. "It was a pardon from the king. For an accused thief. So I stalked that errant envelope to a grassy mound between two tall trees. I crouched like a wrestler as I closed in on it. I was too agitated to worry about how ridiculous this must look—to the coach driver or to anyone else with the good fortune to be watching me.

"As I reached for the envelope, the wind gusted again and my target launched itself skyward, like a startled bird.

It lodged itself in the high branches of the taller of the two trees."

"So of course, you got an axe out of the coach and chopped down that cursed tree?" John offered.

Johannes grinned at him. "So of course I hobbled to that sky-scraping tree and began to climb it like a monkey."

"No, you did not," said Gamaliel, the fishmonger, in mock disbelief.

"I am afraid I did. It took me what seemed like hours, but I grappled my way up that tree. I reached the branch that clutched the letter. I placed one hand on the branch, to brace myself, and I reached for the letter with the other."

Johannes paused for several beats. "As I plummeted toward the ground," he said, "My brain received two distinct messages:

This is going to hurt.

Do not drop the letter containing the king's pardon.

"As to how long I was unconscious, I cannot accurately say.

"At some point, my eyes fluttered open, and I found myself gazing at the fat white clouds with their bruised underbellies. I took stock of my position: Stunned, blinking, and bleeding. Head throbbing and legs dangling at odd angles at the base of the tree.

"I took some comfort in the fact my head was throbbing. That meant my brain was working. So I decided to test my working brain a bit. 'Wiggle toes?' I requested. And my toes moved! I said a prayer of thanks, because this meant two important things:

I was alive

. . . and not paralyzed."

"What about the letter?" the fishmonger asked. "Did you hang onto it?"

"That I did. And when I got out of the Medica . . ."

This brought another eruption of laughter.

Johannes waited for the laughs to surge and then die before he finished the story.

"As I was saying, after I was released from the Medica, I delivered that pardon to a young man named Tarak. I placed the envelope in a small teakwood box tied with a scarlet ribbon. I walked with him out of that graystone prison. We headed down to the water. He opened the box and ripped the pardon into fragments. He tossed them to the wind. The wind carried the pieces away, dancing, dipping, and diving, before finally drowning in the sea."

John pounded his fist on the table, so hard that the mugs and silverware and tin trays shook. "Now that is a story, Climacus!" he boomed. "It is so incredible that it might actually be true."

"It is true," Johannes said. "Only the names have been changed."

CHAPTER 9

THE VIVISECTOR

Johannes had just fallen asleep when he heard the urgent drumbeat of fists on his door.

He stumbled to the door, where he saw Drenda. "Climacus, you need to come down right away," she said. "The Vivisector is here."

Everyone in the Two Kingdoms knew the Vivisector. He was a bloodthirsty swordsman whose name could empty a tavern more quickly than a fire.

"Is he bothering one of the customers?" Johannes yawned.

"He is bothering Regine."

Johannes grabbed his rapier and stutter-stepped down the stairs. "Be careful," Drenda called after him. "Everyone knows he is half-crazy."

Johannes answered her without turning around. "Perhaps I can reason with the *other* half."

The Vivisector had Regine pushed into a back corner. He wore a black shirt, black pants, and soft black boots. His head was cleanly shaven.

"Draw your sword!" Johannes commanded.

The man in black turned around and smiled at Johannes. His face was pinched, as if he had just bitten into a lime.

The Vivisector freed his sword and began carving looping figure eights as he slid toward Johannes.

Johannes stifled a smile. He would rather battle a showman than a warrior any day. He forced his mouth into a thin straight line.

He unsheathed his own rapier and cut a single figure eight but in reverse. He executed the move twice as fast as his opponent—and with greater precision. He saw the Vivisector's Adam's apple bob in his throat, and his shoulders tense. The battle was half won.

The man lunged at him. Johannes danced backward, and the sword's foreswing missed him by an arm's length. When the backswing came, Johannes was ready. He met the edge of the Vivisector's blade with the flat of his rapier. He felt the reverberation of his parry all the way to his teeth, which hummed in his mouth. The man cursed and gathered himself. He took a deep breath and sliced at Johannes with a wide, sweeping arc.

The man in black might as well have announced his move with a trumpet blast. However, as Johannes dodged away, he stumbled backward over a chair. He heard the wood snap and crackle as he landed heavily on it. As he rolled away from the broken wood and tried to regain his footing, he felt the sword slice through his shirt. He waited for the warm and sharp sting of a wound.

He felt it almost immediately.

He popped to his feet, trying to blink the pain from his eyes.

The Vivisector smiled again. There was confidence in that smile. Johannes knew his wound must be significant. His opponent gathered himself once more, then leaped at Johannes.

In one of Johannes's first lessons with Bastien, the knight had told him firmly, "In a sword fight, keep your feet on the ground. Forget what you have read in the books or seen in the plays. Leaping looks spectacular, but it is spectacularly foolish."

Experience had proven the wisdom of Bastien's words, many times. An airborne man has no foundation from which to strike. He cannot change direction in mid-air. And his opponent knows exactly where he is going next. Down.

As the Vivisector began his inevitable descent, Johannes sidestepped his thrusting sword and delivered a clean slice to his opponent's right leg.

The Vivisector bellowed in pain. He looked down at his leg. Blood as thick as syrup was dripping from the wound. He sank to one knee.

"You had better find a doctor soon," Johannes said. "You do not have long."

The man began hobbling toward the door.

"If, by chance, you do not die," Johannes called after him, "know that you are not welcome here."

Then Johannes turned to Regine. "Are you all right?" he asked.

"I am not the one who got my back sliced open with a sword," she said.

Drenda stepped forward. "Get upstairs," she commanded. "I have experience with wounds. I will get you cleaned up. Then we can take you to the Medica."

Johannes felt a grimace of pain spread across his face. He tried to reach behind his back to probe the wound tentatively.

"Excuse me," Regine barked. "What did Drenda say? Upstairs, Climacus!"

An hour later, Johannes heard Drenda say, "Twenty-five!"

Johannes raised his head from his pillow, where he had buried it frequently during the long process. "Twenty-five stitches?" he asked.

"I believe so. They are going to hurt for a while."

Johannes moaned. "*Going* to hurt? My back has been in flames ever since the Vivisector relieved me of my skin."

"Take heart, Climacus. The maidens love scars. And I note that you have several scars. Older scars."

"Not all maidens favor scars," noted Regine, from the doorway of Johannes's room.

"Which sort of maiden are you, Reg?" Drenda asked.

"Which sort do you think?"

Johannes tried to twist his neck so he could see Regine. "My love," he began.

"Silence," she said. "Sleep now. We can talk in the morning. We *need* to talk in the morning."

Drenda placed a dressing over the stitches. She left the

room without comment, snuffing the candles and lamps on her way out.

Johannes lay wide-eyed in the blackness. He tossed nervously in his bed. It seemed that no position could bring him relief. He could hear the restless breathing of the couple in the room to his right. They bickered during the day, and, apparently, their troubles invaded their sleeping hours as well.

The fitful snoring of the guest on the other side amused him. It had amused him since she checked in a week ago. She was a frail young wraith of a woman—who snored like a rooting boar. She had startled him in the hallway twice, because he didn't hear her footfalls when she approached him from behind. But every night she breathed thunder.

Moments later, his thoughts drifted to the Triad. Roth was dead. His friends were wounded but not likely any wiser. He thought about the Vivisector. He wondered if some strange outlaw pride would keep him away from the Medica. Without a doctor, he would bleed out. Or would he? Perhaps the rapier had not bitten deeply enough into that leg.

With some ungainly effort, he wriggled free from the rough sheets and placed both feet on the cold floorboards. He took a deep breath, crouched, and placed both palms against the end of the chest at the foot of the bed. The pain drew tears to his eyes, but he pushed the chest until it rested firmly against his door.

He stood and threw the lock. He frowned. Then he threw the lock again. He slid his feet back toward the bed. It was so small that he feared he might miss it, even in such a tiny room.

It had now been half a year, and still it was almost shockingly strange to sleep this way. No castle walls around him. No knights, ready to take up arms at his command. No Royal Guard who would fight to the death to protect him.

Most nights, he slept soundly, especially after a day of particularly hard work. But every time he or John had to toss a drunk out of the Blackstar, the fear of retribution kept peace at bay.

And the Vivisector was more dangerous than a dozen drunks. If he was still alive.

CHAPTER 10

ANGEL WITH A RAPIER

The next morning, a young doctor visited Johannes. He examined Drenda's stitch-work, pronouncing it "sloppy but effective." He placed a clean dressing across Johannes's back and gave him a brown bottle of liquid medicine. "Take two swallows of this each morning and evening. It will help with the pain," he advised.

After the doctor left, Johannes removed the cap from the bottle and sniffed it. It smelled of cheap liquor. He dared a small sip. The medicine burned like fire. "This is worse than Blackstar coffee," he whispered.

When he had made his way down the stairs, he saw that most of the mess had been cleaned up, with the exception of the splintered chair. Regine was polishing the bar. She walked to the chair and stood over it. He joined her.

"Well, *tektōn*," she said, "can you fix that?"

"I can make something out of it."

"You can?"

"Yes." He smiled. "Firewood."

She pointed to the table closest to the door. "It's an hour before we open," she said. "Sit."

He followed her to the table and sat across from her. Outside, it was snowing, the flakes floating down like tiny white feathers. Johannes pointed at the window. "It is only early fall," he said. "And look what it's doing out there. Only in Denton."

Regine pulled a few errant strands of hair away from her thin lips and sipped her tea. She closed her eyes and smiled.

"Good?" he asked.

She winked at him. "What did a handsome, mysterious man say in my house one day? Like liquid heaven. Are you sure you don't want some, Climacus?"

He wagged his head. "No. Tea makes my nose run. And I realize that I do not have a handkerchief."

She glanced at him. "You can always blow your nose on your shirt. Especially that shirt."

"It once belonged to John," he said.

"Exactly."

"You have something large on your heart, Regine. I can tell."

"I do. It is about your efforts last night. I do appreciate them. As I have every time you have chopped trouble off at its roots since you began working here."

"But . . ."

"But, you and that sword. We both know you are no trouper. But you are no common laborer either. You are a demon with that rapier."

"I like to think I am an angel with that rapier."

"Please do not do that. Dip your words in honey and hope that will make me eat them without question."

"As you wish."

She pushed her tea aside. "King Morgan has his spies," she said. "And they are good ones. But I have my spies too. I know women who can glean more information with a smile than a spy can gather with all his craft and disguises and subterfuge."

Johannes noticed his right leg was fidgeting.

"Women spies," he said.

She nodded. "They tell me that in the capital, a prince is missing. *The* prince is missing. No one has seen him for many months. Meanwhile, many months ago, a mysterious young laborer appears on my doorstep. He does not seem to be a seasoned laborer, but he picks things up quickly."

"Picks things up quickly. That is a good joke."

She made slits of her eyes. "Don't."

She picked up a butter knife and held it up to the light. "Is that rapier your first sword, Climacus? Or did you start smaller?"

He bowed his head. "No. My first sword was a willow switch. One day, I used it to smack a duke across the shins. At least, I think he was a duke. I recall that his green velvet hat sported two white plume roses. They poked out at jaunty angles. So I knew he was someone important. Whoever he was, he limped for the entire week of his visit."

Regine gave Johannes a wan smile. "His visit to the Upper Kingdom?"

"Yes."

Regine exploded to her feet, her hands flying about like white butterflies as she screamed at him:

"Is this some kind of a game to you, Prince? Or is it a bet to win more gold? Is your palace not full enough with riches? I hear that in the Great Hall, the gold bars are stacked like lumber, as high as a man's chest. What kind of folly is this? Did you get bored counting up all your riches, so you decided to ruin a life—on a lark?"

Johannes held his hands toward her, palms up. "I am sorry. But I can explain."

"Explain what kind of name is Climacus?"

"It is my middle name."

"That does not make you any less a liar."

"I know."

She pointed the knife at his throat. "What is wrong with you?"

"I am not good at love," he said. "And it hurts to be so bad at the one thing that means the most to me."

His words seemed to stun her. "Why do you say you are not good at love?" she asked.

"First, I am twenty and seven years old, and I am unmarried. Second, I am shallow. I am a person who lacks depth of character."

"What makes you shallow? Johannes Climacus."

"My inability to receive love."

She nodded. "You are better at giving love than receiving it. I have seen that many times. You need to keep your heart open all of the time. Open to give but also open to receive. That will be my prayer for you. My prayers will follow you all the way back to the capital."

"What if I am not going back to the capital?"

"Don't talk like that. Your game is over. Game. Experiment. Spy mission. Folly. Whatever you choose to call it."

Johannes felt his eyes becoming moist. "Your spies are not as good as you say."

"What do you mean?"

"If they were so skilled, they would have learned that I left the Upper Kingdom for good. I set my royal lineage aside. Our line ends with Morgan the Merciful. Our house will be like the Tudors. Extinct. Perhaps forgotten forever someday."

Regine lowered her knife and spun it on the table. "I do not believe you. You cannot tell me you do not have some princess waiting for you back home. When you have had your fun here."

"I do not have a princess, Regine. And I do not have a 'back home' either. Not anymore."

"If you say so, Your *Grace*!"

The words burned him like acid.

Then Regine grew quiet. She sat as still as a statue, eyes fixed on the wall behind him. Johannes bowed his head and prayed. Prayed for something to thaw the frozen silence between them. "Are you praying, Johannes?" she asked him.

"This is a big problem. And God is big."

"I do not pray to God because He is big. I pray to Him because He is good and kind and loving." Her eyes were moist and shining.

"May I try to explain something to you?" Johannes asked.

"Yes."

"I promise that there is no game afoot here. A year ago, my father and I decided that I should, from time to time, dress as a commoner and visit the cities of the Lower Kingdom."

"To spy on us."

"No. You do not know my father's heart. He truly wanted to know what people thought of him and his leadership. He wanted to know their concerns and their fears. The real ones. Not what the chancellors tend to tell a king. That tends to be precisely what they believe the king wants to hear. Besides, people will tell strangers things they won't tell their own family."

"So you learned much?"

"Yes. I learned things that helped my father become a better king. Things that I knew would help me lead more wisely. Someday. And then I met you. By chance. Here in this inn. You warned me to avoid the venison stew. And I forgot every princess I had ever met. I promise."

"Please. I would not give an iron half-penny for the promises of men."

"What I am saying is true. When I met you here, I knew you had no peer in the entire world. Then, after spending just an hour or so in your home, my life changed. I was back at the palace, but nothing was the same. The kingdom was no longer the past, or even a portal to the past. And it was no longer the home to my future either. Even the bread tasted different. And not a full day had passed."

"This is all so hard to believe."

"I know it is. But it is true nonetheless. And I just realized something: A few moments ago, I told you that I was not sure I had a home anymore."

She sniffed. "I remember."

"But that is no longer true. I know that my home will always be wherever you are. He looked around the inn. This is my life now. You are my life now. And I am in love with this life."

She put her hands in his. "I have much to think about," she said. "How do I know you won't start to miss all of that power and privilege someday? Or start yearning to produce an heir for good King Morgan?"

"I understand your feelings. But I want you to know that my place is here with you. If you will have me."

She withdrew her hands. "As I have said, I have much to think about."

Johannes nodded to her and exited the Blackstar. He stood on the wooden landing outside the inn's front door. He swept his eyes up and down the quiet street. The sky was knife-gray, and the air smelled like burnt biscuits.

He walked a furlong up the main street, then turned and walked back. He wondered how long he would have to walk before something would release the hard knot in his stomach.

He saw Gamaliel the fishmonger approaching. A bushy red beard concealed most of his face, except for his savage green eyes. He had lived half a century, but his body resembled that of an eleven-year-old boy. John called him Beard on a Stick.

Gamaliel stopped and tried gamely to light his pipe in the strong wind. He called down curses upon curses upon the wind.

"Problems, Gama?" Johannes asked.

The fishmonger offered a broken-toothed smile. "I love the wind at my back," he said, "when I am walking or riding my horse. But not when I need my pipe."

"The wind is a fickle friend."

"That it is, Climacus. That it is."

"You should dine with us later today. I will have venison stew."

"I will see you for late supper. Venison, eh? Well, anything but fish."

Johannes laughed politely. "Until later, then, Gama."

Gamaliel bowed slightly. "Until later."

CHAPTER 11

"TELL ME A LIE!"

Johannes spent the rest of the day in a daze. As he worked, tufts of conversation floated by him like clouds. Few words found purchase in his troubled mind. He could concentrate on nothing, save for the questions and doubts that rolled around in his head like marbles. The most vexing questions were these: *What happens to you when you lose the one thing in life that you cannot bear to lose? What happens when your life's greatest dream explodes like a popped soap bubble?*

At lunch, a loud drunk entered the inn, screaming for his wife, whom he planned to beat, for some unspecified infraction. Johannes approached the man and punched him in the nose. He dragged him outside like an animal corpse and returned to the Blackstar without uttering a word.

He saw Regine only once during the workday. He tried to talk to her as she stirred a pot of spiced cider with a long-handled spoon. She shut her eyes tightly and cried quiet tears.

He muttered, "I am sorry," and left her alone.

Hours after the sun had ducked behind the mountains, Johannes told John he was done for the day. He headed outside, to stand in the cool dark. Only a few stars freckled the black velvet sky. He stared down the main street. The street he and Regine used to walk together almost every night after their work at the Blackstar was finished. A gust of wind swelled and nudged a small herd of dead leaves to scratch their way across the ragged cobblestones. He turned and looked at the sign on the Blackstar's front door, penned that morning by Drenda: Music Tomorrow

Nite, it read. Drenda knew how to spell Night, but she didn't like the way her *g*'s and *h*'s looked. In the months in Denton, she had become his second-favorite woman in the world.

Presently, a small train of wagons snaked its way up the street. Someone in one of the wagons hurled a clay mug at him. It shattered against the Blackstar's crumbling stone façade. The noise inspired several dogs to join in an angry chorus of barking. From behind the inn, he heard John's mutt lunging against its chain. John had adopted the dog, a dangerous-looking cur with a lame rear leg, a few months ago. He had named him Quicksilver.

As Johannes stooped to pick up the pieces of the broken mug, he saw a bobbing torchlight approaching him. He stood. The man with the torch drew close, and Johannes realized he did not know him.

"Who are you?" the stranger demanded. His eyes were watery and confused.

"I am the man who would be king," Johannes said.

"You are a king, eh? Well, go ahead then. Tell me a lie."

The stranger walked on, laughing heartily at his own joke.

Johannes contemplated returning to the inn, to see if Regine was inside somewhere. He saw the Blackstar's lamps glowing orange through the windows. He felt nothing glowing inside of himself. His heart felt cold and heavy with dark sorrow.

Chapter 12

Sandor Invades

In the morning, when Johannes went downstairs to begin his work, Bastien was waiting for him. He stood at the bar. Johannes motioned to a table. "Come, sit."

Bastien shook his head. "There is not time," he said.

Johannes frowned. "What is wrong?"

"Much is wrong. The army of Sandor is on its way here. Dozens of ships. Filled with Sandor's warriors. As well as an assortment of thugs, dissenters, and felons of all sorts. Mercenaries."

"Are you sure?"

"When was the last time the king's scouts were wrong about anything?"

"Will they attack both kingdoms?"

"Only the Lower Kingdom, most likely. Old General Desmond knows that the Upper Kingdom is protected by the mountains from the west."

Johannes nodded. "And the trail that cuts through the mountains and then soars to the palace is easy to defend."

"Moreover, that old fox does not know that rust is devouring your father's long-slumbering cannons."

"So it's the Three Cities then."

"Yes. Your father has commanded me to bring you to the palace. Bring Regine. Bring her father. And maybe a couple of your friends. But you cannot stay here. Sandor will cut through the Lower Kingdom like a sword through lard. Even if Bolsta, Hartwell, and Denton were to combine forces, they would be overrun. And we both know there will be no combining of forces. These cities feud and fight like spoiled children."

"My father can send his forces here."

Bas placed a heavy hand on Johannes's shoulder. "He cannot spare the men. You know that Morgan the Merciful has severely reduced the size of the army and the Royal Guard. And we do not know *for sure* that Desmond will not attack us. We must be as ready as possible. Please, Johannes. I have a coach and an extra horse waiting. But you must hurry."

"You know I cannot leave. I cannot flee to save my life while so many here will lose theirs."

"You fail to understand the severity of this matter, my friend. We need you in the Upper Kingdom. We need you to lead. For the past weeks, your father has spent most of his days in the Great Hall, building small gleaming towers with his many coins. He then knocks the towers over, laughs like a loon, and then starts restacking the silver and gold again.

"Yesterday morning, I found him asleep on the floor, by his throne. He was curled up like a cat. When I woke him up, he kept repeating, 'I shall be dying soon.' Over and over and over."

Johannes bit hard on his lower lip. "It is enough to break a son's heart."

"As I said, I have a coach waiting. We can take you, Regine, and perhaps three others. The barman and his woman, perhaps. Decide quickly."

"Bas, I am staying here. I will defend my city. Tell my father that I will visit him straightaway. If I survive."

Bastien bowed his head. "You will not survive. But if you are determined to stay here, I will stay with you."

"No. You will not. This is not your fight. Besides, as you said, Sandor might attack the palace. Get back up the mountain and get ready. Now."

Bastien shrugged. "There is nothing I can say?"

"Nothing. Go."

Johannes watched his friend and teacher exit. He had to duck at the doorway to keep from smacking his head.

It took Johannes less than a quarter-hour to gather Denton's chancellor and the city's most influential leaders in the Blackstar. He outlined his plan for defense, and he sent messengers to Bolsta and Hartwell, warning of the impending attack and asking for help in defending their sister city. Denton was closest to the sea. It would be the first target. But if they put up a stout defense, perhaps Denton would be the only target.

He instructed the vicar of the church to stash the chalices and candlesticks and crosses beneath the floorboards. Bulging sacks of gold were removed from the banks and buried among the trees outside the city.

"If anyone has small diamonds or other valuables," he advised anyone who would listen, "you might consider swallowing them."

Once he had a perimeter defense assembled, Johannes herded women and children into the church and locked the doors. He placed John and Gamaliel outside as guards.

"Do not let anyone get inside," he said.

John swung his heavy sword as if it were a baton. "Count on it," he said. "Regine and Drenda are inside."

CHAPTER 13

DEFENDING DENTON

Near the seashore, just beyond Denton, lived a few dozen families who occupied thatched huts along the beach. They lived quietly, subsisting on fish and seabirds, which they roasted on green spits over low fires. Johannes dined with them from time to time.

The soldiers and mercenaries from Sandor attacked these huts first, killing all but a few who dashed to the temporary safety of the city.

Johannes's and nearly one hundred men waited near the city gates, which he had ordered closed. When the enemy drew close enough, Johannes and his men hurled spears, rocks, torches, and even crockery and metal trays.

Then he signaled to Amos, the inept horn player from the Lonely Dogs, to sound a retreat. Upon the first flatulent horn blast, Johannes's men disappeared into the buildings along the main street, where they prepared for the next phase of their defense.

Meanwhile, the Sandor horde overwhelmed the city gates like a great wave. They poured into the street.

Johannes's men moved to the windows of buildings on both sides of the street. They hurled pots of flaming black powder and poured buckets of lye onto their enemies. Screams of pain followed. The enemy flung their ladders against the buildings. Howling soldiers began scrambling up the ladders. They were met with facefulls of cookware, salt, knives, stones, and the contents of dozens of chamber pots.

Johannes waited at the window on the second floor of the Whetstone. Five men, in turn, tasted the silver fire of his rapier before he sent the ladder crashing to the street below, as another half-dozen enemies clung to it, screaming in terror.

A ragged cheer rose from the men near Johannes, but his face remained grim. Below him, he saw doors being torn from stores, shops, and inns. It wouldn't be long before they were gutted.

With another blast from Amos's horn, the men of Denton fled the buildings and dashed toward the west side of the city. There, Johannes stopped and urged everyone past him. "On to Hartwell," he shouted. "They will be expecting you!"

He hurried to the church, saying a quick prayer of thanks when he saw Gama and John still defending the front door. "Get everyone out, now!" he commanded.

Soon, women and children poured like ants from the front and back doors. Johannes met Regine's eyes. "You know what to do," he said.

She nodded. "I will see you in Hartwell, then?"

"Yes. But go. Go quickly."

He watched Regine lead a church full of survivors out of the city.

He turned around when he heard the thunder of boots approaching. A small band of soldiers sprinted toward the church. They were led by what appeared to be a pirate captain. He wore a deep blue coat, white silk stockings, and gray shoes of soft leather. A long rapier hung from his right side. Its scabbard was covered with silk. Johannes allowed himself a fleeting smile. He wondered how much money General Desmond had parted with to hire a pirate captain as a mercenary.

"You are late," Johannes said to the pirate. "By about one hundred years, judging from the looks of you." He drew his sword.

The pirate glowered at Johannes. "Is your sword as quick as your tongue? You had better hope so."

Johannes made the air hum as he swung his sword and removed a slice of the blue coat. "Nothing below God's heaven is quicker than my sword," he said.

The pirate's hand disappeared into his coat and

emerged holding a single-shot pistol. He aimed the pistol at Johannes's head. He started to speak but stopped when a spear buried itself in his right leg.

Bas rushed forward and disarmed the pirate with his sword. Then he picked up the severed arm and threw it into the midst of the pirate's companions. "Who would be next?" he said.

"Hang it all!" one of them said. "Let's go rob the graveyard."

The small band retreated quickly, apparently not daring to look over their shoulders.

Johannes yanked the spear from the dying pirate's leg and returned it to Bas. He noticed that the front of his friend's tunic was cross-hatched with several long cuts, but only one of them seemed to have drawn blood. And not much blood.

"Bas, I thought I ordered you to return to the Kingdom," he said.

Bas shrugged his massive shoulders. "You're not of the monarchy any longer. I no longer have to listen to you.

Thank God in heaven."

Johannes looked to the east. The army was rolling their way. "Will you run to Hartwell with me, my friend, if I say please?" he asked.

Johannes led his three companions out of the city. As they ran, they began to cough and their eyes began to burn. "Good," Johannes said. "The garbage pits have been set on fire, just as I ordered. And the wind is our friend today."

As Johannes sprinted into Hartwell, he wondered, for a moment, if the smoking refuse had affected his eyesight. But the sight of Braithwaite and the members of the Royal Guard was no illusion. Neither was the sight of at least one hundred of the finest warriors from his father's army.

"Into the city with the four of you," Braithwaite called. "And Johannes, there is a woman waiting for you in the chancellor's office. This part of the fight is ours."

Then he handed Bas a war hammer. "And yours, too, if you want it."

Bas accepted the hammer with a grim smile. "Twin towers forever," he said.

CHAPTER 14

GRAVE ROBBERS

The rout of the army of Sandor took less than an hour. The invaders never advanced as far as Hartwell's city gates. Soldiers and volunteers from Bolsta helped defend their sister city, as did the refugees from Denton.

The defenders then chased their enemies all the way back to their boats. Fewer than half escaped with their lives. From Hartwell to the shoreline, invaders littered the ground, like broken dolls. Shattered swords lay everywhere. One of the king's archers placed an arrow, dipped in the milk of the viper, into the back of General Desmond near the seashore. He died with his face in the mud.

But Johannes could not celebrate the victory. For Denton, his adopted home, was a terrible garden of crimson fire. The Whetstone was a black smoking heap. The Black-star was gone. As if it had never been. The church was a fire-ravaged wreck.

Walking along the main street, and fighting back tears, he saw scavengers poking the ashes with their swords, looking for gold, silver, or anything of value. He was too depressed to crack their heads with the pommel of his rapier.

He found a stunned boy of about sixteen, sitting in a dust-dry pile of ashes near the smashed city gates. He seemed deaf and blind to the swarm of flies orbiting his head. Johannes helped the boy to his feet. "Can you make it to Hartwell?" he asked.

The boy nodded. "Good. You can find aid there. At the Medica. Do you understand me?"

"Yes," the boy whispered.

Johannes tried to rub the smoke-sting from his eyes. He moved on to the cemetery. Tombstones were toppled. It appeared that most of the graves had been robbed of their gold ornaments and keepsakes. Some of the bodies had been stripped of their clothes.

Johannes looked to the sky. The clouds looked like gray ghosts. "I am beginning to understand," he whispered, "why Morgan the Merciful believes there is no such thing as a holy war."

When Johannes returned to Hartwell, the chancellors of all three cities were waiting for him.

"So," said Bolsta's chancellor, "you have surveyed the damage."

"Yes," Johannes said somberly.

"It will take us a long time to rebuild," said the chancellor of Hartwell.

"Us?" Johannes said.

"Yes," said Denton's chancellor. "We have discussed the matter with each city's leadership. The project will begin immediately. Of course, we hope we can count on your help, Prince Johannes."

Johannes shook hands with each man. "Of course I will help. But you should know that I am not sure I am a prince anymore. But I am something of a carpenter."

When Johannes finished speaking, Regine ran to him and threw her arms around him. "You stayed!" she said. "You really stayed."

He returned her embrace. "Of course I stayed. Denton is my home. *You* are my home."

"Thank you for what you did," she said. "John told me that you were a demon with a sword. I told him he was wrong. You are an angel with a sword."

A LEGACY OF SWORDS

The small boy raised his eyes to the sword on the wall.
"That sword looks very old, Father," he said.

"It is," the father said. "It is a bog-iron sword, from
the days of the mighty Vikings. The Vikings learned how to
extract iron from the peat bogs. To do this was very hard. It
took a long, long time. That is why most Vikings, contrary
to the legends you will hear someday, did not own swords.
And most of those swords were reclaimed enemy weapons

from the battlefield. But the bog-iron sword was a real treasure. It would remain in a family for generations."

"Whoa!" the boy said. He pointed to another sword. "What about that one? The sword with the big sharp teeth?"

The father smiled. "I made a trade for that sword, many years ago, on a voyage to the south islands. Long before you were born. It is a Maori sword. Made of wood and edged with shark teeth. The huge one next to it is a war sword from Scotland. It's called a claymore. You need both hands to use it. It is four pounds of almost certain death. But that big long blade came with problems. Two hands on the sword means no shield. And with a claymore, you have only one chance to deliver your damage. If you miss that chance, you, most likely, miss your chance to continue living."

"Is the claymore the best sword of them all?"

The father shook his head. "My favorite sword of all time was one made of Damascus steel. Forged in a crucible. That was a sword that could cut through other swords!"

"Whoa!" the boy said again.

"Damascus steel was forged in a faraway place called

Syria. And how they made such fine steel is a mystery, even to this day. People have tried to make their own Damascus steel. We tried here in this very palace. In a room below this Great Hall, in fact. But no one has succeeded. Yet."

Outside the Great Hall, a woman sat in a garden filled with flowers, some growing from the black earth, others in terra cotta pots as large as wine barrels.

The woman sat on a stone bench in the shade of an oak tree. Squirrels darted around its branches, chittering excitedly. Two sparrows flitted from the top of the tree, seeking adventures beyond the garden's high, ivory-covered walls.

Presently, the woman stood and went inside the Great Hall. She saw her son, standing with his father and pointing up at an Aztec sword, edged with shards of obsidian.

"It is time to depart, you two," she said. "Enough with the swords."

"But I like this palace," the boy said. "And I haven't even sat on the throne yet."

"I like this palace, too," the woman said. "It is a fine place to visit."

The boy frowned for a moment. "This palace was Grandfather's home once, right? Before he died of the Great Sickness?"

The father took the boy's hand. "It was."

"And Grandfather was a king?"

"Yes."

"You lived here, too—and you were a prince?"

"Yes, I was."

"So," the boy said, tapping a forefinger on his lips, "does that mean I am a prince too?"

The woman took the boy's other hand. "Morgan," she said, "you are a prince to *us*." She looked at her husband. "Isn't that right, Johannes?"

"It is. A prince to us. Now, let us go. You can sit on the throne during our next visit. I know King Bastien will not mind. But now it is time to return home. Our coach to Denton is waiting."

As they walked to the coach, the boy said, "Can I ask Uncle John and Aunt Drenda to call me *Prince* Morgan?"

"Certainly," his mother said. "Go ahead and ask."

Late Night with Søren Kierkegaard

Søren Kierkegaard was a man of contradictions. He was one of the most brilliant people to walk the planet, but the faith he held so dear was, to him, not a matter of the mind. In fact, he criticized all attempts to make religion "rational." Further, he was a devout believer in God, but he was almost as devout in his criticism and distrust of the church. Finally, he was a passionate man who believed in true love, but he broke off the engagement to the only woman he would ever love. He never married.

Imagine this controversial genius philosopher as a guest on one of our late-night talk shows. The interview might go something like this:

Host: Our next guest is the brilliant Danish philosopher and thinker, Søren Kierkegaard. Søren, it's a pleasure to have you on the show.

SK: I ask you to avoid labeling me as a philosopher or a thinker. Once you label me, you negate me.

Host: My apologies. All that I meant is that, clearly, you are a guy who understands his faith. Christianity, in your case.

SK: Let other people admire and praise someone who claims to understand Christianity. I consider it my duty to admit that one *cannot* truly comprehend Christianity.

Host: But, Søren, how can you defend your faith if you cannot understand it?

SK: It is stupid to defend Christianity. Christianity is not some miserable something or another that has to be rescued by a defense.

Host: I must say that I don't understand you. You are one of the smartest people in history. Are you saying your brains have nothing to do with your faith?

SK: I am saying that nobody can attain religious faith by any objective examination of the evidence. My being a Christian is a subjective choice. It is a leap of faith. I must add that the amount of objective evidence supporting one's belief does not necessarily make those beliefs genuine or true. True belief is measured by sincerity and passion. I criticize all attempts to make religion rational. God wants us to obey Him, not argue on His behalf.

Host: But doesn't growth as a believer in any religion require learning and thinking?

SK: A learner becomes a believer when he sets Reason aside and receives the deeper understanding of the Eternal. Faith cannot be distilled from even the sharpest accuracy of detail.

Host: Well, I guess that Christianity does have some content that could be considered unreasonable. Take Abraham and Isaac, for instance.

SK: I find Isaac's near-sacrificial death fascinating. You see, God sometimes requires His believers to hold beliefs and perform acts that are ridiculous, or even immoral, by human rational standards. I admire Abraham for obeying an outrageous command—without trying to understand or justify it. Abraham was a true knight of the faith.

Host: Speaking of faith, let's talk about church for a bit. You were quite critical of your country's major church, the Danish Lutheran Church.

SK: What can one say of a church that assumes all Danes are Christians simply by virtue of their birth? In my view, the Danish Lutheran Church contained no true Christians. Other than that, I have no critique.

Host: Moving on, then, I am wondering how you feel about the state of today's morality. People are doing some very bad things.

SK: People have always done very bad things. And true sorrow for one's sins is no more rare today than it was two hundred years ago. Where is the deep sorrow for the sin itself?

People seem to show sorrow only for sin's consequences, the shame and the disgrace. We must show true repentance and remorse for the wrong we do. Then we must will the Good with all purity of heart.

Host: So maybe people haven't changed much over the years. But do you think God has changed over the course of history?

SK: God is not history. He is not the past, nor the future. He confronts us *right now*. The present tense is the only one that matters.

Host: You are one intense guy, Søren. I like you, but you are a little strange.

SK: I am strange. I am a stranger in a strange land. To be a follower of Jesus is to be an alien. You must not surrender your soul to society, and that means not even to the church.

Host: Really? But doesn't the church—

SK: I am telling you: You must pursue an authentic and individual encounter with your Lord. You must build an *authentic relationship* with Him, a relationship that is deeply personal. Do not follow any institution—including the church—that tells you what your relationship with your Lord should be. Do not let another person tell you what that relationship should be. Pursue the relationship that is honest for you. This is between you and God. Be an individual before God. Do not be one of those . . . what is the modern word?

Host: Clones.

SK: Amen.

Host: Can a person truly have a close relationship with a figure so majestic and mysterious as God?

SK: The most intimate of all relationships should be each individual's relationship with God.

Host: Is that true for you, honestly?

SK: I confess that it is hard for me to explain my own God-relationship. My God-relationship is the happy love of my life, but this love has been, in many ways, unhappy and troubled. This might seem a contradiction to you, but such is the nature of all true love stories.

Host: I am guessing that prayer is a big part of your relationship with God. Do you truly believe that God listens to all of your prayers? And does He answer them?

SK: Prayer does not change God. Prayer changes Him who prays.

Host: Our time is almost up, but I can't let you go without a couple more questions. First of all, you are such an intelligent guy, but I can't get over the way you downplay the importance of thinking.

SK: I do not downplay thinking. I merely distinguish a turning of the mind from a leap of faith. What we think *is* important, because our life always expresses the results of our dominant thoughts.

Host: And isn't it our thoughts that keep us from believing in God?

SK: No. It is so hard to believe in God because it is so hard to obey Him.

Host: I think more people should obey God. After all, He created the whole world, didn't He?

SK: Yes, God created the world, out of nothing, but He did something even more wonderful than that. Something He does every day. He creates saints out of sinners.

Host: I think that is one of the most beautiful things I've heard in a while.

SK: The highest and most beautiful things in life are not to be heard about, nor read about, nor seen. The most beautiful things in life, if one is willing, are to be lived.

Host: Any final words of advice to our viewers out there who would like to do better in their duty to God?

SK: Yes. Duty to God will never cause you to cease to love. No knight of the faith should ever cease to love. Love always, and do not forget to love yourself.

A SØREN KIERKEGAARD
TIMELINE

1813   Søren Kierkegaard is born in Copenhagen, Denmark. His mother is 45; his father is 56. (In all of his many writings, Søren will never directly mention his mother.)

1830   Søren, age 17, enrolls as a theology student at the University of Copenhagen.

1838   At age 25, Søren publishes his first book, titled *From the Papers of One Still Living*. The book is a critique of the fiction work of Hans Christian Andersen.

1840   He becomes engaged to Regine Olsen. She is only 17, 10 years Søren's junior. A year later, Søren will break off the engagement, fearing that his melancholy nature will make him an unsuitable husband.

1841   He successfully defends his doctoral thesis, which is titled "The Concept of Irony with Constant Reference to Socrates." While he wrote the thesis in Danish, he defends it in Latin. For the next 10 years, he does little else but write and wander the streets, talking with the "common people."

1843   Søren publishes *Fear and Trembling*, a book exploring the biblical story of Abraham and Isaac. He found Isaac's near-sacrificial death fascinating. Søren argued that God sometimes requires His believers to hold beliefs and perform acts that are ridiculous, or even immoral, by human rational standards. The book lauds Abraham for obeying an outrageous command without trying to understand or justify it. He calls Abraham a "knight of the faith."

1846   Publishes the book *Concluding Unscientific Post-script* and pursues plans to become a pastor. *Concluding Unscientific Postscript* argues that nobody can attain religious faith by any objective examination of the evidence. It is a subjective choice, a leap of faith. He added that the amount of objective evidence supporting one's belief does not necessary make those beliefs genuine or true. True belief is measured by sincerity and passion. He criticized all attempts to make religion rational. God wants us to obey Him, not argue on His behalf, he asserted.

1849   Publishes four books, including *The Sickness Unto Death*.

1850   Begins a public attack on the Danish Lutheran Church, calling it a "state church," which assumes that all Danes are Christians by birth. One of the vehicles for this attack is a series of self-published periodicals called *The Moment*. He asserts that the Danish Lutheran Church contains no true Christians.

1855 Publishes *The Changelessness of God* and *What Christ Judges of Official Christianity*. He also continues his controversial attack on the Lutheran Church. On a cold day, he collapses on the street, perhaps due to stress. He dies in a hospital a few weeks later, on November 11, at age 42. Most biographies attribute his death to "spinal disease."

CAST OF CHARACTERS FOR
A KING IN DISGUISE
(in order of their appearance)

Roth – charter member of the Triad (a band of thieves); rough-looking; black teeth; sharp-boned; at least forty-five but looks ten years older; carries a sword; usually drunk; bulging belly

Johannes – a twenty-seven-year-old prince; heir to the throne of the Two Kingdoms; son of Morgan the Merciful; wears a silver cross, given to him by his mother who died; very good with a rapier; goes by his middle name Climacus to disguise who he really is; willing to give up throne for the woman he loves

Brooks – second member of the Triad; plump and powerful as an ox; moves like an ox, too; has jowls and a mashed-in nose; carries a club

Red Face – newest member of the Triad; tar-black hair; red face; thin; wears only a knife on his belt

Two-Finger Tomas – former member of the Triad; now sitting in jail of the Upper Kingdom; every few months someone from the Triad is jailed, executed, or converted to faith

Eron Denton – a quarryman that the city of Denton is named after

Regine – red hair; dark eyes; proud nose; high cheekbones, like her father; sharp wit; not fond of the monarchy

Truman – Regine's elderly father; white hair; high cheekbones; wise

Bastien – the knight who taught Johannes the art of battle; very tall

Morgan the Merciful – king of the Two Kingdoms; Johannes's father; sad brown eyes

Braithwaite – another member of the Royal Guard; very tall; he and Bastien are known as the King's Twin Towers

John – serves drinks and maintains order at the Blackstar; "thick bear of a man"

Drenda – serving woman at the Blackstar; black hair and white skin; "voice like molasses"

Morgan the First – Johannes's grandfather who was king before Morgan the Merciful

Gamaliel – a fishmonger in Denton; staying at the Blackstar; bushy red beard; savage green eyes

Tarak – character in a story Johannes told at the Blackstar; he received a pardon from the king

Vivisector, the – half-crazy and bloodthirsty swordsman

Quicksilver – dog that John had adopted; has lame rear leg

General Desmond – leads the attack on the Lower Kingdom from Sandor

Amos – horn player from the musical group the Lonely Dogs

About the Author

Todd Hafer has written more than 50 books, which have sold more than 2 million copies. He lives on the Kansas plains with his family and his wayward rescue dog. He is very grateful to his elder son, T. J., who educated him on sword lore for this book. For more information, visit haferbrothers.com, the official website for Todd and his taller (and more talented) brother Jedd.